PUFF...
CURIOUS TALES F...

Shaguna Gahilote is a performance storyteller. She is a maths wizard with a double master's degree, having studied in both India and the UK, where she was a Commonwealth Scholar. She came back to India to work on conserving rare and dying folk art forms. She has worked as an education, peace and culture specialist and helms Ghummakkad Narain: The Travelling Literature Festival and Kathakar: International Storytellers Festival, now in its tenth edition.

Shaguna spends her days writing, drawing cartoons, solving maths problems with her nephew and looking after her pet Labrador, Ginger, as well as her neighbourhood strays. She has trotted around the world on a staple diet of potatoes, eggs and hummus.

Prarthana Gahilote has been a journalist with the national media—spanning print, TV and digital platforms—for over two decades, with a stint in the UK as a Chevening Scholar. She is the festival director of Kathakar: International Storytellers Festival, India's first and only oral storytelling festival.

Prarthana suffers from wanderlust and loves walking in the Himalayan forests whenever she can escape her homes in Delhi or Mumbai. When not occupied with the alphabet, she is found spinning yarns with family and friends, pampering her nephew, Raghav, and her pet, Ginger. She has an ever-growing collection of books, fountain pens and antiques. She directs short films, documentaries and digital concerts. She also writes poetry in Hindustani as well as lyrics for songs. She can't live without music or gulab jamuns.

Besides writing stories together, Shaguna and Prarthana are often found chasing their adopted rescues turned pets, Matru, Tchoti, Bucky, Romi, Bella, Jackson and Jerry. Their love for animals has led them to be founding members of an animal welfare trust, Animals Are People Too—a Mohit Chauhan Initiative, which looks after over 350 stray animals across India, feeding and providing medical care to stray animals, especially dogs. Shaguna and Prarthana take pride in calling themselves 'dog slaves'. To know more about them, please visit www.gahilotesisters.com.

PRAISE FOR THE BOOK

'An unpolluted and fresh breeze of Himalayan tales—intriguing and insightful. A wonderful collection of stories that sheds light on our folk tales and mythology, and provides an understanding of nature and life in the Himalayan region'—Vishal Bhardwaj

'A charming and thoughtful evocation of the very special magic of Himalayan folk tales'—Namita Gokhale

'The scent of the Himalayas is in these pages—silky and spicy stories that take us back to the primitive exuberance within us'—Imtiaz Ali

'A rich repository of the innate wisdom and beauty of the Himalayas. Fascinating and perceptive. A must-read—for those who love the Himalayas and have been there and for those others, longing to be there'—Mohit Chauhan

Curious Tales
from the
Himalayas

SHAGUNA GAHILOTE
PRARTHANA GAHILOTE

Foreword by His Holiness the Dalai Lama

Illustrations by Jit Chowdhury

PUFFIN BOOKS
An imprint of Penguin Random House

PUFFIN BOOKS

USA | Canada | UK | Ireland | Australia
New Zealand | India | South Africa | China

Puffin Books is part of the Penguin Random House group of companies
whose addresses can be found at global.penguinrandomhouse.com

Published by Penguin Random House India Pvt. Ltd
4th Floor, Capital Tower 1, MG Road,
Gurugram 122 002, Haryana, India

First published in Puffin Books by Penguin Random House India 2017
This edition published in Puffin Books by Penguin Random House India 2022

Text copyright © Shaguna Gahilote and Prarthana Gahilote 2017
Foreword copyright © His Holiness the 14th Dalai Lama 2017
Illustrations copyright © Jit Chowdhury 2017

ISBN 9780143428602

Typeset in Cochin LT Pro by Manipal Technologies Limited, Manipal
Printed at Replika Press Pvt. Ltd, India

www.penguin.co.in

Papa, 'Ab ke hum bichde to shayad kabhi
khwabon mein milein.'

*To Pa, who unveiled the world of words to us, and Amma, who
taught us how to decipher the magic that lay there.*

*To Raghav, who encouraged us to cook up stories for his
childhood, turning us into storytellers, and Ginger, who peeks
through many of these.*

And to Rachna, our constant source of love and support.

'The Gods who made this land must
have been beauty-drunk'

—Paul Brunton, *A Hermit in the Himalayas*

Contents

THE DALAI LAMA

30 September 2017

Endorsement

Our sense of human values is passed down by various means, one of which is folktales. Folktales help preserve the popular wisdom that sustains our human society with love and care. This book contains folktales from the Himalayan region, which will, I am sure, allow readers to take pleasure in its rich culture. I commend the authors - two sisters - Prarthana and Shaguna Gahilote for their good work.

With my prayers and good wishes,

Introduction

The stories in this book have been chosen to bring a certain flavour of the Himalayas to the reader, and have been hand-picked from the western, central and eastern Himalayan belt to cover every range. Some of these tales are very popular, others rare and a few—once popular—are now lost to the new generation. Some stories here have been reproduced from childhood memories, while others, whose details were lost, had to be researched and many others were found during our travels and treks in the mountains!

There is no one tale that can be described as the first version ever told, or one that forms the basis of all other folk tales. As people travelled along the Silk, the Incense and the Spice Routes, they carried with them folklore and folk tales. So, a story that one might have heard as a child in a village in India could be a folk tale from England or Russia, because these fables have travelled across the world since ancient times and have been adapted to each country to suit its cultural ethos.

As we researched the stories for this book, we found varied versions of the same tale spanning many different regions. We've tried to stick to the one we believe is the most relevant. For some, missing portions were pieced together from other versions.

Folklorists around the world believe that folk tales prepare children for the future, which is why life's darkest lessons are told through demons and witches. These supernatural beings in the stories may be manifestations of people's inhuman emotions. Older tales have evil stepmothers and stepsisters, a reflection of those times, when women would often die during childbirth, and children had to grow up to face a cruel world, moulding their own lives as they grew up. Folk tales were woven with so much mystery and magic, always ending in happily ever after, that the lessons were conveyed without being preachy.

And then there is the perennial discussion regarding folk tales having too many graphic and gruesome details. Should we be telling stories of evil parents, uncles and aunts to children, or should we spare them the nasty details, like those in 'Tejimola', 'Lakshi, Dulal and the Monkeys' and even 'Hansel and Gretel'? Psychologists explain that children have their own interpretation of these stories and understand them differently from adults. They absorb the essence of a story without getting consumed by the macabre details. This is why tales have to be told without adding 'So the moral of the story is' at the end. Of late, folk tales are being pushed to teach values and morals to kids in an obvious way, and need to be freed from this restriction. Stories need to be told as stories, free of any labels, so that children can imagine them as they like.

Stories are constantly being lost; parents heading nuclear families have little time to tell tales to their children, and technology has given kids many other tools to interact and engage with. But stories have a shelf life far longer than any fads and trends do. Stories last for generations, reviving themselves around campfires, spitting up flames, hibernating during the winter and blooming again with the sun in spring—spreading like the fragrance of the rhododendrons in the Himalayas for anyone who wishes to drink them in and share!

The Red Fox and the
Meditating Monk Frog

Nubra Valley, Ladakh

The winter in Nubra Valley was rather hard this year. The snow gods had been working overtime to ensure every blade of grass in the upper Himalayas was buried under. Mountain bases were just as white as their peaks, and the rivers had started to freeze. The town of Leh had been shut down for the winter. This happened every year when the frost set in. Supplies couldn't get to the town's residents, leaving them with no choice but to pack their bags and leave or ration every last resource they had gathered in the previous months.

The birds had been forced to fly southwards, looking for warmth and food. Their wings allowed miles of travel, and they had begun their journey even before the first of the flakes drifted down from the sky. By the time the ground turned white, the only creatures left were the ones who couldn't hibernate by digging a hole in the soil. The rabbits and rats were away, hidden. The marmots had stocked up enough fat and dug themselves deep into the ground. Even the ants had lined up in their safe haven, deep under the freezing sand.

The older foxes and wolves had been a worried lot since last year. There had been signs of how cruel the coming winter would be, and they had told their offspring that if they hunted in good time, they would be prepared for winter. The younger foxes, busy strutting around to impress potential partners, had paid little attention to this advice.

The shortage of food became apparent at the beginning of the season. With the smaller animals all hidden away, the red foxes started climbing down the mountains in search of food. During this descent, they would fight amongst themselves in a bid to destroy any competition for food in the villages. Many of the villagers kept animals for their own use. The cows were well fed and soft, and they were slow to duck fox attacks because of the comfort and protection the villagers gave them.

Even the guard dogs in the village were not very ferocious; they had fought only amongst themselves and had little experience of real brawls. The cats were so pampered by their owners that they rarely managed to give a good chase to the foxes. All these were the best bet for hungry foxes looking to satisfy the fire in their bellies.

Foxy, a handsome four-year-old, was left alone when his parents lost their fight to the stronger foxes in their area. Foxy was scared and alone for the first time; he now needed to look after himself. He had seen the Nubra Valley with his parents, full of flowers in the summer. They had told him then that in winter he would have to go down to the valley with them in search of food. But the cold had been half a year away then, and he hadn't bothered asking them much about the road to Nubra. Now, the mountains were covered in ten feet of snow, making the walk down a very tricky one for Foxy.

He had never thought that he'd be making this journey alone one day.

Foxy was worried about the bigger foxes he knew he would run into—he didn't want to fight them. The bigger foxes, thankfully, didn't consider him a match for their strength and skill. As Foxy walked down, he looked back longingly at the mountaintops, his home, where he had spent his time howling and playing. It was a distant dream now.

The village looked deserted, which was a good sign for Foxy. He looked around abandoned settlements for any morsels of food. There was a chance that the humans, looking to save themselves, might have left behind the older animals that were incapable of making long journeys. But there were no animals in sight.

Foxy walked around, but nothing could be found. At the end of the valley ran a stream. Thinking some water would moisten his parched throat, he hopped up to it. The stream was completely frozen, with not a drop to drink. Foxy was saddened because he had thought a little water would also fill his rumbling stomach. He walked up and down the stream, searching for a chink in the ice. He must have walked a mile when he heard a soft gurgle coming from close to a rock. The ice there was thin, and Foxy thought that this could be where he'd find a strip of water. He hit the ice with his paw. It gave way and a large patch of water opened up. Foxy bent down and gulped hungrily. As he drank, he noticed something from the corner of his eye—a bright green blob behind a pebble. Foxy bent down to look closely and moved the pebble with his paw. Whoosh! Flying out on to the ice came a fat green frog!

The frog landed on the other side of the river. Surprised by Foxy's sudden invasion, the frog jumped up and climbed on to the nearest rock. Foxy was thrilled! Food, finally. He started walking towards the frog, ready to gulp him down.

'Who dared to wake me from my meditation?' the frog croaked in his deep voice. It echoed through the valley. He stared at Foxy, demanding an answer. Foxy was amazed. Meditation? That's a word he had heard before. Ladakh was full of Buddhist monks. Foxy had met them on his way and seen them around their campfires, as they travelled across the great Himalayan belt, preaching and chanting. But in his entire life, he had never come across a meditating frog. Could this be a human monk who had transformed himself into this creature with his spiritual powers? Or was this a frog with miraculous abilities? Foxy didn't know.

As Foxy looked puzzled and frightened, the frog croaked again, 'Who had the guts to wake me from my deepest meditation, and at a point when I was about to meet the Buddha and find my enlightenment?'

Foxy, scared, squealed for forgiveness, reaching out to touch the frog's feet. As he was doing so, he suddenly wondered if the frog was lying. What if this was just an ordinary frog hiding itself from the winter cold and now trying to save himself?

Foxy thought he'd try a trick of his own. He drew back, raising himself to his maximum height, and growled, 'How come a monk as great as you was cowering behind a small pebble? I have seen and met revered monks on my many travels in the mountain desert, and I know that all of them meditate as humans. You show me your true human self, and I will let you go.' *This is a clever condition*, Foxy thought smugly. But his happiness was short-lived. It dawned on him that if this frog really was an old monk, he'd surely punish Foxy for his insolence.

The frog was smarter. He had met many hungry foxes before, so he wasn't afraid. He deepened his voice and croaked, 'You unbelieving beast! It is your ignorance that makes you wander these mountain ranges so aimlessly. If you had some sense, you would have found the Buddha in your many years of travel.'

Foxy was confused. He had encountered many people on his travels who looked like the Buddha, and some who spoke like the Buddha. Every monk was a Buddha in his eyes. So which Buddha was the frog talking about? He growled, 'I have already met many monks and never needed any of them. I have been hungry for many nights, so all I need is food. You will be my meal today.'

Though Foxy had tried his best to be menacing, the frog realized that his gut feeling had been right. The handsome young fox clearly did not have much experience in hunting, or he would never have revealed his hunger so quickly.

The frog rasped, 'You think I am a frog and have no powers. I would have transformed into a monk and punished you, but I cannot, as I need to complete my meditation. So I shall show you my powers while remaining a frog, and then you shall leave me alone at once.'

Foxy wondered what abilities a frog could have and said, 'I am ready to challenge your powers, little frog.'

'I challenge you to jump across this great river, if you dare,' the frog responded. 'The one who jumps the farthest will be crowned the winner.'

Foxy remembered all the long jumps that he had been trained to do by his parents. He thought this would be easy, for no frog could jump farther than a fox. He took a few steps back and readied himself for a leap across the river. As Foxy leapt into the air, the clever frog jumped on to his back and grasped Foxy's fur with his hands, feet and mouth.

Foxy was a champion long jumper. He flew across the river and landed on the other side. The frog, who had been clinging on to Foxy's back, used that moment to loosen his grip and leap from Foxy's back to a spot farther away.

Once on the ground, Foxy looked around to see where the frog was. His eyes rested on a spot far ahead of him. Foxy was bewildered. How had the frog jumped so far?

The impact of the landing made the frog cough. As he spluttered, he spat out a clump of Foxy's fur.

The frog saw Foxy's bewildered expression and said, 'You look surprised to see the fur in my mouth, but don't worry. This is from a big snow leopard, who was as nasty as you are. I was about to sink my teeth into him, but then he grovelled for forgiveness and promised to bring me food every day. He should be here any minute.'

By now, Foxy was convinced of the frog's mystical powers. He sought forgiveness from the frog. Afraid that the frog might curse him if he stayed longer, Foxy fled.

Disappointed, Foxy, starving and worn out from his leap, started the journey back. On the climb up, Foxy met a snow leopard. Seeing how tired and defeated Foxy was, the snow leopard asked him what was wrong. Foxy narrated the entire episode with the magical frog. Old and wise, the snow leopard guffawed and said, 'I've lived in this region for years and have never seen or heard of a meditating monk frog. I often go to the river to drink water, and no frog would ever dare to challenge me.'

The snow leopard told Foxy to come with him to the river so that they could teach the frog a lesson. Foxy's embarrassing story worried the snow leopard. If the frog

was not taught a lesson, no small animal would ever again obey the commands of a larger beast.

Not completely convinced but scared of defying the snow leopard, Foxy started to follow him down to the stream. The leopard babbled, 'This winter has been the harshest of the past ten years. There's no food to be found anywhere. No animal will be able to survive without food. Not even a fly or a frog.'

Suddenly, the words of the frog came back to Foxy. A snow leopard had been spared certain death on the promise that he would get the frog food every day!

Foxy froze. This must be a trick. The snow leopard would take poor Foxy straight to the frog for his dinner and perhaps even gorge on the leftovers. In a flash, Foxy took off as fast as he could.

Surprised, the snow leopard ran after Foxy to get him back. Down at the stream, the frog saw the silhouettes of the leopard and the fox, and thought to himself that it was not his turn to be somebody's dinner—it was the fox's.

They say that even today foxes can be seen running in the western Himalayan belt, holding their tails tightly between their hind legs. If you do spot one, you know it's the one running away from the monk frog and his disciple, the snow leopard!

This folk tale is from the Nubra Valley in Ladakh. However, similar tales are found in Tibet and even as far as Bhutan. In some stories, the leopard is replaced by the fox, and the challenge between the frog and the fox is either more complicated or even simpler.

The Bowl of Thenthuk

Hemis, Ladakh

A ngchok and Rigzen were celebrating their fiftieth wedding anniversary on the fifth of this month of February. The cold and barren desert of Hemis, where they had lived ever since their wedding day, was what they called home. Rigzen was a resident of the village Phey, a little distance from Chilling, before she was married to Angchok. The tiny village of Chilling didn't have many people living in it, but it did have an abundance of wildlife. Wolves, bears, eagles and even majestic snow leopards — Chilling had them all.

In the fifty years of their marriage, Angchok and Rigzen had rarely spent a day without each other. Their two children, Tashi and Jigmed, had been sent to live with their uncle in the city of Leh, many miles away from Chilling. They had gone to school there and, once educated, had both moved out of Ladakh to further their careers. Their hectic lives allowed them little time to visit their parents. So Angchok and Rigzen kept each other company.

The winter months were particularly demanding in Chilling. Like most mountain households, families worked extra hours during the summer to prepare for the snow-laden winter, and they stored up necessities like food, firewood and meat. The challenges of the winter did not just arise from the sub-zero temperatures in the region but also the unavailability of work. To compensate, the summer months would see the villagers working overtime in their fields, reaping the crop and drying a share for winter. No one would ever risk being unprepared for the winter months.

Left to their own devices in Chilling, the elderly couple just about managed to get by. Like most village people living in rough conditions, the couple made money through various odd jobs. There had been a time when both Angchok and Rigzen were young and could do a lot of work in the house, in the field they owned and even at the little shop that Angchok would set up in autumn to sell woollen socks, scarves and shawls that Rigzen had knitted. But of late, business at the shop was erratic because Rigzen's old fingers couldn't manage much knitting. The housework was always divided between the two. Angchok would go out to the forest and collect tinder for the evening fire. This wasn't an everyday affair, but when it had to be done it required hard labour. Rigzen would tidy the house and prepare the couple's meals. And they would both tend the field and grow enough potatoes and almonds to tide them over the winter months.

One crisp morning, Angchok was on his way to the forest to collect some firewood, when a neighbour urged him to go to the village square first. Angchok's neighbour, Dolma, was rushing to the square for a hurriedly called meeting of the village folk. As Angchok started walking with Dolma, she told him that Tenzin, a village senior, had spotted a snow leopard close to the village boundary. 'It was huge! As big as the apple tree,' Dolma exclaimed.

'Tenzin *∂ai* saw it when he came out of the house for you-know-what,' she giggled. Many of the villagers weren't entirely convinced of ninety-year-old Tenzin's report, due to his failing eyesight, but news of a snow leopard close to the village, even if it was purely imaginary, could not be ignored. With winter at its peak and the upper reaches of the region cut off, the snow leopard's possible arrival was a worrying development. What could have brought the beast down from the forests? Had he just strayed and lost his way? Or was he too old to hunt and had come to the village in search of food?

Round and plump Dolma's face was flushed. Part of that colour came from her nervous excitement, and part of it came from her laboured and hurried walk. Her red cheeks added to her childlike innocence, which nobody, including Angchok, could ignore. They arrived at the square, and Angchok listened to more and more exaggerated tales of the leopard—how huge he was, how fast he ran and how many animals he had snatched up. Since the spotting of the snow leopard, the story about him had changed many times, with each villager trying to outdo the other. While the spotting of a snow leopard was serious business, it was also some sort of entertainment. Especially since this gave the grey-haired residents something new to talk about.

A little while later, Rigzen too was called to the square. The couple sat next to each other, listening to what was being said. Some villagers said there were two leopards, a male and female together. Others said it was an old one, well past his hunting heyday. And someone said that their sheep dog had started to howl when the leopard entered the village. Each version got more exaggerated and bizarre. When these stories started being repeated, Rigzen and Angchok thought it was time to get going.

Rigzen started her walk home, and Angchok went to the forest to collect kindling. At home, there wasn't much for Rigzen to do. Her house was sparse and, since she and her husband were the only occupants, there wasn't a lot to clean. But out of habit, Rigzen went about scrubbing and dusting the house. Once she was done inside, Rigzen's mind wandered to the winter stockpile. She went out to look at the dried produce stored in the barn. Most of it had been consumed in the past few months. She had only a small amount of thick, flavoured noodles left to cook, and the very last of the dried meat. Dried vegetables might last the winter, but they'd have to say goodbye to the meat and thick noodles.

With the sun up, Rigzen dragged out the worn rugs and woollen clothes from the house. She would dry them outside, as the warmth of the sun worked as a disinfectant. Rigzen hung the rugs on the top of her boundary wall and took the woollen clothing to the roof. Her thoughts strayed to the commotion that the snow leopard had caused in the morning, so she looked around from the height of the roof to see if she could spot anything in the forest. Thankfully, there was nothing unusual to be seen.

By now, Rigzen was tired, so she decided to rest a while. The balmy late morning and crisp wind had made her very drowsy. She climbed down from the roof, stretched out her legs and began to doze. But a rustle in the tall grass behind her jolted her awake. The thought of the leopard petrified her, but once again, there was nothing to be found. Everything seemed fine. She went back to sleep, lying so still that a passer-by could have mistaken her for dead. What the poor old woman had missed in the camouflage of the light-brown grass was a pair of yellow eyes, watching her every move. Rigzen would be easy prey.

Meanwhile, Angchok was on an exhausting trek. He had been collecting dried branches and twigs since late afternoon. He was too old to climb the trees and cut off branches, so he had to make do with picking up fallen twigs.

The entire morning had been spent listening to tales of the leopard. The early afternoon had gone in climbing up to this clearing. Now, Angchok had only a couple of hours to collect enough firewood to last him a few days. Under his breath, he cursed himself for listening to Dolma and following her to the village square. If he hadn't done that, he wouldn't be rushing himself now.

Once enough wood had been collected, Angchok put it on the ground and undid the cord tied around his waist, which was otherwise used to hold together his long Ladakhi wool coat. This cord, worn by many Ladakhis, would often come in handy for odd jobs outside the home when things weren't readily available. Now, he used this cord to tie the bundle of twigs he had gathered. He started the trek back home. This walk back was even longer than the climb up. On Angchok's back was a huge bundle of wood that pushed his spine towards the ground. Hunching under the heavy weight, he walked slowly and carefully down the mountain slope.

Back home, it was late evening when Rigzen roused. Dusk had given way to darkness, and she was surprised that Angchok hadn't returned. Rigzen realized that she needed to hurry to make their dinner. She quickly lit the evening lamp, collected the rugs and decided to get the clothes from the roof once she had put the thenthuk on the fire. Rigzen was starving, and the delicious noodle soup, with its succulent chunks of mutton and hearty vegetables, would really hit the spot.

As the shadows of the trees started blurring in the fading light, Angchok finally arrived at the foothills.

From here he could see a dimly lit settlement—his village. Home was still far, and the weight of the bundle was too heavy, but the sounds of the forest made him quicken his pace.

When Rigzen hurried into the house, she left the barn door open, knowing that she would come back to store the woollens there. The thenthuk wouldn't take too long to make. All she had to do was put the dried noodles into a pot of water, mixing in the balls of dough, vegetables and dried mutton.

As she prepared the food, Rigzen realized that Angchok was very, very late. Her mind started racing. What could have caused this delay? Could it be the leopard? She tried to banish the thought, but it kept coming back. To distract herself, Rigzen decided to dump the clothes from the terrace into the barn. She'd arrange them in the morning.

While Rigzen was putting the clothes away, the sumptuous smell of the boiling thenthuk wafted over to her. Afraid that she might burn it, she hurried into the house, forgetting to shut the barn door. Though she had wanted to wait for Angchok, Rigzen could hear her stomach rumble. She couldn't hold back her hunger any more. She ladled her portion into a bowl and ate it all up.

Angchok had still not arrived. The fire was crackling, and the simmering thenthuk was almost boiling over. Just as Rigzen was about to put out the flame, Angchok arrived with a huge bundle of firewood. Exhausted from the walk and the weight of the wood, he dumped the bundle by the wall and almost slumped on to the floor.

Rigzen brought him a cup of warm water, but what he needed was food. He was in a bad mood, so Rigzen quickly poured the thenthuk into Angchok's bowl and handed it to him.

'Be careful,' started Rigzen, but Angchok swatted her away. 'It's very ho—' she started to say, when she saw that Angchok had already put his lips to the bowl. 'Hot, hot, hot!' cried Rigzen, but it was too late. The soup burnt his lips, mouth and throat.

In anger and shock, Angchok spat out the thenthuk. 'You crazy woman!' he screamed, and threw the bowl at Rigzen.

Shocked by Angchok's reaction and hurt by the unexpected missile, Rigzen squealed, 'I was warning you!'

'Didn't seem like it! I think you were plotting to kill me,' yelled Angchok. He picked up his axe, waving it around. 'I'll get you before you do away with me! Get out of my house! Get out of my village! Get out of my valley! Don't be seen in Hemis ever again,' Angchok shrieked.

Look at this senile old fool, thought Rigzen. She knew she wasn't at fault. So why should she take Angchok's insults? 'You ungrateful beast, you'd better watch out. I'll kill you. I'll chop you up and throw you to the hungry dogs. You'll regret coming back to the house!' she hollered, throwing pots and pans at him.

'Ha! As if you would ever dare! I'll be the one doing the hacking. You'll be nothing more than minced meat soon. Don't think I'll let you get away. I'll whack you with my stick and slay you with my axe,' barked Angchok.

That night, they say, there was so much noise from the belligerent old couple that the entire village was woken up. Their shouting and cursing echoed through the wilderness of Hemis, and the villagers gathered to see what was wrong.

In the barn, snug in the corner where the cattle's hay was stacked, the snow leopard had been startled awake by the clatter of the bowl thrown at the adjoining wall. He had been waiting in the barn all evening, hiding quietly and hoping to snatch up the old woman. He had planned on getting her in the backyard, but she woke up before he could attack. His second chance had been to pounce on her from the grass when she was putting away her clothes, but he had failed when she suddenly rushed out of the barn and into the house. It was then that the snow leopard saw the open barn door and decided to wait for Rigzen inside. But the warm hay and cool breeze had lulled him to sleep.

Now, having been shaken awake by the terrible din, he could hear words like 'kill', 'chop', 'hungry dogs' and 'minced meat'.

The snow leopard thought that the old couple had discovered that he was hiding in the barn and was planning to kill him. He got to his feet and, as he trained his ears to the commotion outside, heard the marching of hundreds of human feet walking towards him. The snow leopard froze, thinking the whole village was getting ready to slaughter him. He remembered old man Tenzin spotting him the night before. He had come down to the village hoping to find some food, but it looked like he was the one who would end up being dead meat.

The leopard realized that he had to escape the village and run far, far away, where fierce warriors like Angchok and Rigzen did not live. He leapt out of the open barn door and sprinted towards the jungle, away from the villagers, who were making their way to the old couple's house. As they arrived at Angchok and Rigzen's front door, ready to placate them, they were alarmed to see huge paw prints on the ground. Immediately, everyone stood alert, scanning the area for a leopard. It was old Tenzin who saw the fleeing animal. 'There! Leopard!' he bellowed, as the villagers let out a huge cry.

The snow leopard panicked on hearing this deafening bellow, and he doubled his speed. With a few more leaps, he landed outside the village boundary and disappeared into the jungle for good. The villagers were convinced that the leopard had run away thanks to Angchok and Rigzen. Had the old couple not cooked up this cacophony, the leopard would not have run away. With a loud cheer, they burst in on Angchok and Rigzen, yelling, 'Bravehearts! Bravehearts!'

The snow leopard was never seen in the village of Chilling again. It is said that even now, ages after Angchok and Rigzen unwittingly scared away the snow leopard, the big cat runs for its life when it hears human footsteps.

As for Angchok and Rigzen, they lived comfortably in their village for the rest of their days, never again having to look for food, firewood or warm clothes. They had been declared village heroes, and the other residents had taken it upon themselves to provide for the couple for the rest of their lives. Though they weren't sure what they had done to deserve this special treatment, Angchok and Rigzen certainly weren't complaining. With their silly fight now in the past, they never raised their voices at each other again, and the couple lived happily ever after with the blessings of a scared snow leopard.

This folk tale from Hemis is one of the most popular tales in Ladakh. Ladakhi kids might not remember other stories from the region, but they would have heard this one from their grandparents. And while they might not be able to remember all the details, they never forget the couple's fight over the steaming bowl of thenthuk.

Kaala Paaja

Himachal Pradesh

Sukhiram and his son, Kirnu, had lived in the small village of Vashisht all their lives. Kirnu's mother, Devi, had passed away while giving birth to Kirnu. When Kirnu was very young, Sukhiram would leave him in the care of helpful neighbours and go to the neighbouring town of Manali to find work as a daily wage labourer. His employment and his earnings were erratic. He would return to Vashisht every evening to look after Kirnu and play with him. Sukhiram's meagre wages would be spent in buying food for Kirnu and himself. Sadly, he had no money to give Kirnu a comfortable life. Sukhiram's neighbours were kind people, and they would feed Kirnu during the day but would also tell Sukhiram that he needed to provide more because his son was growing and required more care and attention.

Sukhiram knew that the neighbours were right and meant well, but there was little he could do to better his situation. So when Kirnu turned ten, Sukhiram took him to a nearby ashram and handed him over to a very old sadhu called Guru Kapish.

Kirnu started working in the ashram and following Guru Kapish with great care. In very little time, Kirnu became the apple of his guru's eye. Guru Kapish was known for his meditation and mantras. He had rare spiritual powers that had found him fame in Kullu Valley. People from as far as Tibet came to seek his blessings. It was said that anyone who came to Guru Kapish was blessed for life and relieved of all their troubles.

Ever since Kirnu's arrival in the ashram, Guru Kapish had become fond of the innocent little boy. Kirnu was a very cute child. He had red cheeks and dark eyes. Every time Kirnu was happy or his stomach was full, his eyes would twinkle. The twinkle could be seen at least twice a day, once in the morning and again in the evening, when Guru Kapish would call Kirnu to eat with him. Kirnu would lick and slurp from his bowl, devouring with relish the sweet rice that was given to him.

When Kirnu turned fifteen, Guru Kapish felt that it was time for him to start learning the sacred healing mantras that he had known all his life. So began the guru's tutelage.

Many years went by, and Kirnu's guru kept training him. One day, when Kirnu was meditating, Guru Kapish sent for him. The guru said to his pupil, 'Kirnu, today I have turned 100 years of age. You have also grown to be thirty. It is now time for me to retreat to the jungles on the top of the mountain and for you to take charge of the ashram. When dawn breaks tomorrow, I shall leave the ashram for good.'

Kirnu was shocked. He had never imagined that his guru, his only friend and constant companion, would ever leave him. Kirnu's own father had only visited him twice a year, till two years ago, when he had breathed his last. But Guru Kapish had never left Kirnu's side. How could he abandon him now?

Kirnu started crying and told Guru Kapish, 'I won't let you go. You can't leave me. If you go, I will go with you. If not, stay here and let me serve you.' Guru Kapish tried hard to explain to Kirnu that he could not stay in the ashram any more. His education in mystical sciences did not allow him to stay in the ashram after he turned a full 100. Kirnu refused to listen and held on to his guru's feet. He stayed there, his arms wrapped around Guru Kapish's legs the whole day and then the whole night. When dawn broke, Guru Kapish woke Kirnu up and told him he was going to get ready to leave the ashram. Kirnu started sobbing and told his guru, 'I'll only prepare for your departure if you let me come with you, or else I'll throw myself into the pond and end my life.' Guru Kapish loved Kirnu and finally agreed to take him along.

An hour after dawn, once the guru and his student had bid goodbye to all the other disciples in the ashram, Guru Kapish and Kirnu started walking towards the top of the mountain. The forest wasn't very thick when they started their journey. But after two hours of walking, the guru and his shishya encountered forests so dense that it was difficult to take even a single step. The duo realized that this part of the forest was unexplored, and wild creepers had made a web of green in between the trees.

By afternoon, Guru Kapish and Kirnu decided that they must move south to find the Beas river. They would walk along its banks to keep themselves from losing the way. This would be an easier journey than their current one.

A few hours of walking southwards brought Guru Kapish and Kirnu to the Beas. The sight of the clean, flowing water brought much delight. They were exhausted. Guru Kapish turned around to look at Kirnu, who was following him, and said, 'Do you think we should stop here a while and cook some food? It's almost sunset, and it will be easier to light a fire now and cook some khichri.' Kirnu hungrily imagined eating the hot rice and pulses mixture, and he nodded in agreement. Guru Kapish added, 'Perhaps after that we could make ourselves a grass bed here.'

Kirnu found some kindling to light a fire, and Guru Kapish started preparations for the meal. He told Kirnu to go deeper into the forest to get more firewood to keep them warm through the night.

When Kirnu headed into the forest, Guru Kapish walked to the river to wash up. The water was cold and clear, and it tasted rather sweet, like mountain rivers often do. He then pulled out a small pot from his cloth bag and collected some water in it — just enough to cook the rice and dal in.

As the khichri started to cook, Guru Kapish sat on a rock and observed the rushing river. The constant gurgling of the river, sounding like the ascending whistle of a wild thrush, the yellow sky and the mellow evening sun, ready to set after a hard day's work, were all so magical. He was transfixed. He hadn't seen an evening as beautiful as this within the confines of his ashram. He sat there for a while and then walked to the fire. Since the flame was small, the khichri was taking time to cook. The guru realized that it needed stirring, so he looked around for something he could use as a ladle.

His eyes fell on a stick floating in the Beas. He walked up to the river and pulled out the sturdy black stick. He figured that the stick was a good substitute for a spoon, and so he scrubbed it clean and started stirring his khichri with it. The meal would take another half hour to cook, so Guru Kapish started his evening meditation.

When his eyes opened, the sun had already set, and there was a deafening clamour of birds winging homewards. The guru looked around for Kirnu. Not seeing him anywhere, Guru Kapish thought he'd check on the khichri. He wanted it to be ready by the time Kirnu returned. When he looked into the pot, Guru Kapish was horrified. The khichri that had been bright yellow was now completely black. Black as a moonless night. Black as charcoal. Black as a mountain crow! Guru Kapish could not believe it. How had it burnt? After all, he hadn't meditated for that long. The khichri didn't even smell scorched. Suddenly, it struck him. Of course, the culprit was the black stick. Parts of his temporary ladle must have dissolved into the khichri, turning it black. Guru Kapish pulled the stick out of the pot and immediately flung it into the river.

The guru was upset that his food looked so rotten now. And Kirnu would come back, tired and famished, to a ruined meal. Guru Kapish couldn't bear the thought of serving this inedible meal to Kirnu, who had always taken special care of him.

The guru decided to eat up the whole pot of black khichri, so that Kirnu would not even see the remnants of the spoilt food. For Kirnu, he thought, he would cook a fresh pot of khichri so that he could have a hearty meal.

After eating every last morsel of khichri, Guru Kapish hurriedly washed the pot clean and started preparing more food. He let the pot sit on the flame without stirring its contents this time.

The khichri was done just a few minutes before Kirnu arrived. Guru Kapish saw his disciple and heaved a sigh of relief. As Kirnu walked towards where he had left his guru, he seemed unsure in his gait. Even from a distance, Guru Kapish could tell that Kirnu was uneasy. The guru said to Kirnu, 'What took you so long? I was worried. Hurry and wash up. The khichri is ready.'

Kirnu was taken aback. His face turned pale, and he stumbled back. 'Who are you? How do you know about the khichri? What did you do to him?'

'Him? Who him?' asked Guru Kapish. 'Are you all right? What are you talking about?'

'My guruji. Where is he? What did you do to him? Where did he go?' Kirnu demanded.

'What? It's me—your guruji. Don't you recognize me? What's wrong with you, you silly lad!'

'Are you mad? What, you think I wouldn't recognize my guruji? You think I don't know my guruji? You're crazy!' Kirnu spat out.

Guru Kapish was stunned to hear his disciple speak to him so disrespectfully. And how could he not recognize him? Perhaps some spirit or ghost had entered Kirnu when he was looking for firewood. Or maybe his ravenousness had driven him to eat something in the jungle, which had now caused him temporary amnesia or even madness. He walked up to Kirnu and gave him a hard shake. Kirnu freed himself from Guru Kapish's hold and jumped back. 'Don't you dare touch me, you stupid boy,' he screamed.

'Boy? Me, a boy?' Guru Kapish shot back. 'Not even you are a boy any more, you grown-up fool of thirty.'

That was it. Nobody had ever called Kirnu a fool. He was infuriated.

'No juvenile like you will get away with insulting me,' he said and pulled Guru Kapish towards himself. 'Let me show you.' Kirnu aimed his fist at Guru Kapish's face.

The guru was shocked. In all his time with Kirnu, he had never seen him this angry or violent. He pleaded, 'Beta, what has happened to you? Don't you recognize me?

Did you eat something toxic in the forest, or do you not want to be my student any more?'

Exhausted by this conversation, Kirnu began to cry and said, 'I'm so tired. All I want is for my guruji to be with me. Please don't play games with me. Please just tell me where he is. I beg of you.' Kirnu was now sobbing, choking on his own words.

Seeing Kirnu cry, Guru Kapish started to sob. As tears ran down his cheeks, he put his hand on Kirnu's and said, 'Look at me, son. I am your guru. Please accept me.'

'How can I accept you as my guru? Just look at yourself,' said Kirnu, pulling Guru Kapish to the river. On any other day, this kind of behaviour would have brought Kirnu a punishment of three days without food and three days of continuous meditation. Today, however, outside of their ashram and in the wilderness of the forest, everything had changed. Kirnu found a still pool of water next to the riverbank, and he pushed his guru towards it. He would be able to show him his reflection in this.

Guru Kapish bent over the puddle. He let out a scream when he saw his face. Staring back at him was a teenage boy, about fifteen years old, with tight, radiant skin and thick black hair. He almost fell back with shock and fright. The guru looked at Kirnu in disbelief.

'What has happened to me, son? What has happened to me? Oh God, what is this?' he wailed. Kirnu looked even more distraught. He had no idea what had happened to his guru. But then, it dawned on Guru Kapish, as thoughts of the black khichri began to swim in his mind. 'Khichri! Khichri! Khichri!' yelled the guru.

'Khichri?' asked Kirnu, completely bewildered.

'Yes, the khichri,' exclaimed Guru Kapish. He narrated the story of the black stick and the khichri to Kirnu. When he finished, he said, 'Kirnu, there's no doubt in my mind that the black stick that I used as a ladle was *kaala paaja*, the magical herb found in the high reaches of the Himalayas. It causes age reversal. It had to be that. There is nothing else that could have turned an old man of 100 into a young lad of fifteen.'

Kirnu fell at his feet. 'Are you sure? Are you sure you are my guruji? And if you are, are you sure that it's not some magic mantra that has made you so young? Please tell me the truth,' Kirnu pleaded.

'I am your guru, son. And I do not know any magic mantras for age reversal. If I did, I would have told you about it. I've never kept a secret from you. Never. Since the first time you looked into my eyes and called me Baba.'

The only people who knew about this special nickname were Kirnu, Guru Kapish and Kirnu's late father, Sukhiram. No other person could have known it. 'Guruji, Guruji,' cried Kirnu, collapsing, 'I'm sorry for how I behaved. Please forgive me.'

The guru and his pupil hugged each other and wept. In one evening, everything had changed for them. Kirnu finally turned to Guru Kapish and said, 'Guruji, please give me some kaala paaja so that I too can become younger. How can I, your disciple, be older than you?'

Guru Kapish shook his head. 'I can't. I was afraid you might not like the black khichri, so I ate it all and threw away the stick.'

'We have to find the ladle then. We have to!' said Kirnu.

'Let's try,' agreed Guru Kapish, and the duo started looking for the herb. For hours after sundown, the two searched for the black stick on the banks of the river. But nothing was found.

As night fell, the two fell asleep next to the Beas, exhausted from the trials of the day. That night, Kirnu's mother, Devi, came to him in a dream and softly said, 'I was the one who made Guru Kapish find the kaala paaja, a rarity of the Himalayas. I thought you would both eat it. Your ages would be reversed and then you'd be with each other forever.' Devi was worried for Kirnu. She had thought that Guru Kapish, now 100, would die, leaving Kirnu alone. She wanted her son to be with his guru for as long as possible, and kaala paaja was the only way out.

But living forever is not something that fits into the Creator's scheme. Everything that is ever born must perish, and everything that ever comes must go. That's how the water of life keeps flowing. Before she faded away, Devi said, 'You and your guru are blessed and pure souls. If you look hard enough, you will find the kaala paaja again. You are destined to.'

On hearing about the dream the next morning, Guru Kapish said, 'God has sent us our purpose through your mother. We must now travel and look for the kaala paaja. This will be our eternal journey together. The kaala paaja she sent us is not merely about becoming physically younger. It stands for our endless quest for knowledge.'

Even today, they say, wandering shepherds sometimes see a young boy and an older man walking around the forests of the Kullu Valley, looking for kaala paaja. Very often, the wafting smell of khichri follows them wherever they go, especially when they are close to the river.

Those luckier and more discerning even hear their muffled sobs and soft footsteps at sunset. The guru and his shishya haven't found the kaala paaja, but their eternal voyage and quest for knowledge continues.

This folk tale is from Rohtang, which is in the Manali tehsil of the Kullu district of Himachal Pradesh. The region has been home to many sages, like Vasistha, Vyas and Bhrigu, who all meditated along the Beas river. It is believed that in the Himalayas grow herbs with miraculous attributes, like kaala paaja, which cause age reversal and longevity. Many believers have spent their lives walking in the mountains, searching for these herbs.

Kali and Ghughuti

Uttarakhand

After a long and extremely bitter winter, when the sun finally shone on the balcony of the royal palace in Rajapur, the capital of the Chand dynasty of Kumaon, it marked a few long-awaited beginnings. This Makar Sankranti, the fourteenth day of January, was going to be special. King Kalyan Chand knew this as he heard the first spirited cries of his child, born to him after many years of a childless marriage. This morning, the crying of the baby echoing through his palace was a sound he could have heard over and over again. But he wasn't the only one happy to hear the baby cry.

Kali, a crow, had been waiting for the arrival of a royal baby in the kingdom of Kumaon. For over 800 years, Kali had been living under a curse, banished to a life of ugliness and humiliation by his guru. Kali was once a lovely crow, as beautiful as a swan, with the elegance of a peacock and a voice as sweet as a koel's. Kali, now the butt of people's jokes and insults for his harsh voice and intimidating appearance, once commanded respect amongst both birds and humans for his wisdom. He lived in the peaks of the Nanda Devi mountain range, where his guru had meditated, prayed and fed him. But now, he had to survive in the lower hills of Almora and eat leftovers from human kitchens. It was hard to compare the Kali of the past with the Kali of today. His beauty and elegance were gone, just like the reverence people once had for him. All that remained was his guru's curse.

Kali remembered every minute of the day he had been cursed like it was yesterday. It had been a clear spring day. Kali was summoned by his guru and told to fly to the distant western peaks of Kamet in Chamoli to fetch him a pot of a rare liquid. Kali's guru had dreamt of this pot and explained to Kali exactly where to find it. As he was about to embark on his journey, Kali's guru said, 'Come back with the pot intact. Remember not to consume even a single drop of the liquid from the pot or a terrible curse will fall upon you.'

It took Kali a long time to cover the distance to the peaks his guru had told him about. He went past the Nanda Devi range and beyond in search of the pot of liquid. After two weeks of flying, Kali arrived at Kamet and, following his master's instructions, found the pot of liquid. The flight to Kamet had been a long and arduous one, and Kali was tired. He'd had no break because his guru needed the pot before the season changed. Kali bent down to pick up the pot and, tempted to quench his thirst, sipped a few drops of the liquid. He then started his journey home.

When he reached the sage, Kali lowered the pot at his feet. But the guru was enraged. Through his powers, the guru had discovered that Kali had sipped a few drops of the rare liquid. Smouldering with anger, the sage said, 'You insolent fool. You dared to disobey me. That was amrit you tasted, the elixir of eternal life, and it was meant for me! Go now, you will lose all you have!'

'I only had two drops, Master, because I was thirsty.'

'Yes, and now I banish you to a life of ignominy. May you lose your sheen, may you croak, may you eat leftovers and may you never find anything but ridicule.'

Kali was dejected to hear his master's words. He sat at his feet and wept inconsolably.

'Go away! Go away!' his master kept yelling, but Kali remained there, sobbing. A little later, when the sage's anger ebbed, he felt some pity for Kali and told him, 'I can't take my curse back and you will lose all your virtues, but you will be able to keep the wisdom that you gained over so many years with us here.'

'Master, I don't want beauty or grace. I don't even want a musical voice. But how will I live a life being humiliated by all humans and birds? Please do something. Please. I didn't mean to defy you. Show me some mercy!' Kali pleaded.

The guru's heart melted, for he saw remorse in Kali's eyes, and he recalled all the years Kali had served him as an honest disciple. Finally, he said, '800 years from now, when you will be living in the lower plains, wait for the day when King Kalyan Chand has a child.

That day will mark a change in your life and will bring you respect and honour from all humans. Once every year, on the same day, they shall celebrate you.'

Now, as Kali heard the little prince cry, he thought, *My day of deliverance has come*. The bird perched himself on the prince's window and took a long look at him. He was a beautiful baby, with red cheeks and twinkling blue eyes. His mother, cradling him in her arms, kept singing to him, 'Ghughuti! Ghughuti, my little baby.'

King Kalyan Chand organized a massive feast and week-long festivities to celebrate his son's birth. The prince was showered with gifts from everyone who came to see him. He was given toys, special fabrics, sweets and shoes, but what the prince loved the most was a necklace of rubies gifted to him by his grandmother. The little prince refused to part with it and would start crying every time his mother tried to take it off his neck.

Soon, his mother began to use the necklace to stop the prince from crying. Whenever the prince would start wailing, the queen would tell him, 'Ghughuti, stop crying or I will give your necklace to the crow outside.' Ghughuti would look at the bird perched outside the window and stop crying immediately. Quietly, an unspoken bond was being built between Ghughuti and Kali. The crow would watch over Ghughuti from his perch for hours, and Ghughuti would look at him for entertainment.

A few months after Ghughuti's birth, King Kalyan Chand summoned all his courtiers. In the presence of his prime minister, he told them, 'Today, you have been gathered for a special reason.' The courtiers stood attentively as they waited for their king to make his announcement.

'All of you know I have been blessed with a child after many years. I had given up hope of ever having an heir, and had made a few decisions regarding the future of this kingdom. Today, I must announce what I have planned for my people.'

The prime minister waited with bated breath. A year ago, the king had called him and said, 'Your family has always been loyal to the Chand dynasty. I worry about the kingdom, for there is no one after me to carry on our legacy.' The prime minister had quietly looked on as the king added, 'I therefore hand over the reins of this kingdom to your able son, who shall be king after my death.'

But since the birth of Prince Ghughuti, the prime minister had been worried for his son. His fears were confirmed when the king announced, 'I declare that after my death, my son, Prince Ghughuti, will be crowned king.'

The prime minister was furious. His whole world had come crashing down. As soon as the king left for his chambers, he stormed out of the court and met his supporters, a group of men who had been waiting for the prime minister's elevation. Together, they hatched a plan to kidnap the prince and murder him so that the prime minister's son could become the ruler of the land.

The morning after the announcement was made, the queen came out of her parlour to dress her son for the day. But she didn't find him in his cradle. Thinking Ghughuti might be with his father, the queen walked to the king's room. There was no one there.

Perhaps he's taken Ghughuti to the queen mother, she thought. But she didn't find him in her room either. This was worrying—where could the prince have gone this early in the morning? She called the guards and asked them to look for Ghughuti, and then went in search of the king, panicky and afraid.

The king was in the temple with the queen mother, discussing a puja that needed to be done by the royal priest for the young prince.

'The prince! The prince!' the queen wailed when she spotted her husband from a distance.

'What happened to him?' the king asked, shocked.

'I can't find him anywhere! I have looked all over and told the guards to do so too. He's disappeared!'

'How could that be? I saw him in the morning when you were getting ready. Where could he have gone?'

'I don't know! Just find him for me. I can't live without him,' the queen wailed.

The king dashed towards his court. There, he told his ministers and guards to search the palace grounds and find his son. In no time, the palace was buzzing with soldiers. The highest officials of the kingdom were out looking for the prince. No nook or corner was left unchecked, no stone left unturned, but there was no sign of the prince.

After hours of combing the palace and the town, when the prince still could not be found, a soldier in the royal balcony was drawn to the constant cawing of a crow sitting outside the window of Ghughuti's room. The crow had now been cawing for what seemed like hours, and the soldier, assigned to check the private rooms of the palace, recalled hearing him even when he began his hunt in the morning. He looked outside and saw Kali desperately calling for his attention. In his claws he held what seemed to be the prince's favourite necklace. Promptly, the soldier climbed on to the windowsill and released the necklace from the crow's feet. He took the necklace to the king, who recognized it as the prince's.

Encouraged by his ministers, the king decided to go to the balcony and find Kali. As soon as Kali saw the king, he flew off.

The king shouted, 'Follow the crow! I think he's telling us something. Since he had the necklace, he might know where the prince is.'

The king, his ministers and the soldiers mounted their horses and galloped behind the crow. Kali made sure to remain in sight, so that the king's entourage wouldn't lose its way. He flew eastward from the palace and led the team to the thick of the jungle on the hillside. Kali seated himself on a high branch. When the king caught up with him, he ordered his soldiers to climb to the branch and look for the prince. Right below them, deep in the middle of a hedge and hidden from passers-by, Ghughuti lay in the grass, surrounded by other crows who seemed to be guarding him. From the branch, the soldiers clamoured, 'There he is! The prince is right there!'

The king rushed where the soldiers were pointing. He cut through the bushes till he could see his son. But he wasn't prepared for what he saw next. Hidden in the undergrowth next to the prince were five soldiers from his own army, ready to attack the king.

When the king approached the soldiers, they pulled out their swords and started attacking him. The king's contingent immediately sprang into action, and captured the rogue soldiers.

The king cradled Ghughuti in his arms and hugged him so tightly that the prince woke up from his sleep and began to cry. Remembering what the queen would say to Ghughuti when he cried, the king said, 'Ghughuti, stop crying or I will give your necklace to the crow!' The royal entourage erupted into laughter.

The troops returned to the palace, and Prince Ghughuti was handed over to his mother, who fell to her knees when she saw the boy. The five captive soldiers were interrogated, and admitted to kidnapping the prince on the orders of the prime minister, who was planning on killing the boy. When the king was given this news, he knew what he had to do.

Meanwhile, the queen was so overjoyed to see her son that she insisted on rewarding Kali. 'If he hadn't shown us the necklace, we never would have found him,' she told the king. The king and his ministers agreed. After all, it was Kali who had guided them to Ghughuti and protected him with the other crows.

When the king announced to his people that the prime minister was being given the death sentence for kidnapping the prince and attempting his murder, Kali pecked at the prime minister's head repeatedly, till he

was locked up, almost as if to avenge the beloved prince's kidnapping.

To reward Kali, the queen suggested organizing a feast for the crow and his friends. 'I want to give them a treat. I will prepare balls made from flour and jaggery, and string them into a necklace. I want Ghughuti to wear this necklace and offer the biscuits to the other birds as a sign of our gratitude,' she said.

The very next day, the king informed his servants of the queen's plans. The entire kingdom of Kumaon joined the royal family in their thanksgiving. Every household in the realm prepared the flour and jaggery balls and got their children to toss them in the air for the birds to eat.

That day, true to his guru's words, Kali and the other crows regained their lost reputations. They were now admired as wise and loyal birds, and were revered for saving Prince Ghughuti's life.

Ever since, every year on Makar Sankranti, the fourteenth day of January, the people of Kumaon offer cookies to the crows, not just as a sign of gratitude but also as a mark of their faith that the birds will protect their children from evil. To this day, flour and jaggery balls can be seen flying in the air every January.

This folk tale is from the Kumaon region of Uttarakhand. The story is still relevant to the people of Kumaon who garland their kids and present sweets to the crows in their region on Makar Sankranti. Another version of this story has a slightly different plot — King Ghughut was cursed to die on Makar Sankranti at the hands of a crow. He ordered the entire kingdom to make biscuits made from flour and place them on the far side of the palace, thus distracting all the crows.

Yet another says that the king's adviser, called Ghughut, planned a rebellion against him, and the king was informed about the adviser's plan by a crow, allowing him to crush the rebellion in time. Since then, the king ordered that on Makar Sankranti, only crows would be treated with good food. Some also view the festival and the offerings to the crows as a gesture to welcome migratory birds to the region. Another myth says that crows still come to a region in Kumaon, higher up in the mountain ranges, to achieve nirvana.

Tears of Blood

Tibet

A long time ago, along the Yarlung Tsangpo river, there was a mighty kingdom with a benevolent ruler. He had five beautiful daughters, who took after their mother. They were kind and took great interest in the affairs of the palace, along with their parents. The time came for the first daughter to get married, but the thought of losing his child overwhelmed the king. He realized that each of his daughters would eventually get married and leave for faraway kingdoms. He started to worry for his subjects. Who would look after them when he died? He had to have a son to rule his kingdom. These concerns engulfed the king and bothered him day and night. The king's prime minister couldn't bear to see his ruler so worried, and advised him to visit the Great Monk who lived on the top of the mountain along the southern bank of the Yarlung Tsangpo river, in order to consult him about his restlessness. The Great Monk was a disciple of Guru Rinpoche and was said to have magical powers like his guru. He could cure anybody of any illness, mental or physical. The prime minister assured the king that the monk would solve his problems.

The king, taking the advice of his prime minister, started on the journey to the Great Monk's abode with his queen. He travelled for fourteen days, over mountains and through valleys, crossing streams and rivers to meet the Great Monk. When the king reached the monastery with his entourage, he was greeted by the monk at the gate, holding a bowl of water. The king, joyous on seeing the monk and crippled with exhaustion, fainted at the feet of the Great Monk. The monk asked for the king to be carried to a room and allowed to rest. The next day, the king asked for an audience with the Great Monk, but his request was denied. He asked again the next day but remained unsuccessful in his endeavour. Days passed, yet the king's request was unfulfilled. He remained at the monastery, waiting to speak to the Great Monk.

One day, as the queen was strolling along the monastery's boundary, she met a beggarwoman at the gate. The woman looked like she hadn't eaten in weeks. Her hair was matted and her skin coarse. Upon seeing the woman's dishevelled state, the queen called her staff to assist her and provide for her. The queen ensured that she was cleaned up, given new clothes to wear and fed well. The beggarwoman remained with the queen's staff for the rest of their stay at the monastery, and the queen personally looked after her.

On the fourteenth day after their arrival, the Great Monk called the king and queen to his chamber. The Great Monk was lighting the butter lamps in front of Avalokiteshwara—the giant statue of the Buddha—one by one. The royal couple bowed before the monk, but before they could say a word, the Great Monk said, 'Do you think that if I don't light these butter lamps, the Buddha would live in darkness?'

The king was surprised by the question and said, 'No, how can the Buddha be in darkness?'

The monk asked, 'Then should I be consumed by the worry of lighting up this monastery?'

The king shook his head and said, 'No, I suppose not.'

The monk replied, 'Then why should you worry so much about who will take care of your people after you? The one who will take care of the light here will be the one who takes care of your people.' The monk motioned for the king and queen to leave and sat cross-legged in front of the Buddha to meditate. The king was baffled about how the monk knew about his troubles but found peace in the monk's words of advice. He prepared to leave the monastery, after giving the monks a huge offering of precious jewels and gold coins.

As the staff readied for their journey back home, the queen asked the beggarwoman to join them in the palace. The woman declined, saying, 'I have always lived here; this is my home. I shall not leave this place.' She thanked the queen for her generosity and, just before bidding the queen farewell, said, 'You've been very kind to me. I am a beggar and don't have anything to give you, but I must warn you that once your son turns fourteen, you have to watch out for the stone tortoises outside the palace gates. If their eyes turn red, it's a sign that a great flood will swallow your kingdom.'

The queen was very confused and disturbed by what the woman had said. *My son? But I don't have a son! And what is this great flood? What about the tortoises? We don't have any such tortoises at the palace gates,* she thought, deciding to tell the king about this upon their return.

When they reached home after the long and tiresome journey, the queen fell ill. Her daughters tended to her, and the palace physician was called to her bedside.

The physician had good news to share, that of the queen's pregnancy. The news took over the palace and the kingdom. Shortly after, the king and the queen were blessed with a son. The whole kingdom rejoiced at the great news. For a whole fortnight, festivities took place in the kingdom. The king was thrilled, and distributed food and gifts to his people. Royal families from other kingdoms travelled long distances to see the newborn prince, bringing with them rare rubies, corals and pearls as presents. After all the celebration had died down, when the king finally got some time to himself, he thought of the Great Monk and his last pilgrimage. Overcome by a sense of gratitude, he thought of making another trip to the Great Monk, to thank him for his blessings. He wanted to leave for the Great Monk's monastery as soon as he could, but the queen reminded him of the upcoming wedding of their second daughter, and a few more weeks went by. Since the king was unable to go to the Great Monk, he arranged for gifts and annual contributions to be sent to the monastery. Many summers passed but the king did not manage to meet the Great Monk, even as the yearly donations continued.

As time passed, the prince turned thirteen, and the king decided to crown him the heir apparent and hand over certain administrative charges as a mark of duty. To commemorate the grand occasion, the city was adorned, and princes from nearby kingdoms arrived with invaluable presents. A celebratory mood took over the realm. The day the king crowned the prince, gifts were distributed to all the residents of the kingdom, scrolls were painted and two commemorative statues were placed outside the palace gates. The king and his family walked around the palace to greet their guests. But when they reached the palace gates, the queen took one look at the new statues and fainted. Two tortoises stood guard on either side of the gates.

The king panicked and immediately called off the celebrations. When the queen regained consciousness, she burbled, 'Statues. The tortoise statues. Remove them. Remove them.' The king was puzzled. His subjects, out of their love and as a symbol of longevity, had erected the statues of the tortoises for their future king's well-being. But the statues reminded the queen of the words of the beggarwoman all those years ago. She told the king about what had happened at the monastery. The king felt distressed, and he prepared to leave for the monastery to consult the Great Monk.

Once again, he made the arduous journey, travelling across the great mountains and passes, valleys and meadows, brooks and streams, and reached the monastery, with his staff and son in tow. He inquired about the beggarwoman, but nobody seemed to know or remember her.

The Great Monk granted them an audience at the end of their third day there. The worried king started to narrate his tale, when the monk interrupted and said to the prince, 'Come, son, help me pack my bag.'

The little prince did as he was told. The king became restless after a while and started to narrate the story again, but the monk interrupted, 'My disciples and I have decided to pack our bags and leave the monastery.'

The king was confused and asked, 'But why, Great Monk? You have a beautiful home here and you are all so well taken care of.'

'Change is the only constant in life. I have lived here for very long and have been very comfortable, but in a year's time, all this land will be immersed in water, so

I must migrate and prepare in advance for people who might come to me for help,' replied the monk.

'Holy One, then is it true that there will be a great flood next year? What should I do? How should I help my people?' the king asked.

'Your kingdom will not be flooded until the tortoises' eyes well up with red tears. You and your people are safe till then,' the monk responded.

'Holy One, please be kind to us. Only you can help us, so save my people,' pleaded the king.

'As I said, the flood will not come till the tortoises' eyes turn red. But you've been kind to your people and to the monks; you will find greener pastures beyond the flood.' Saying so, the monk bowed, picked up his belongings and left with his disciples.

The king should have been worried, but the monk's last words to him gave him some comfort. He returned to his kingdom and discussed everything with his family. They could not tell their subjects about the flood, as there would be complete hysteria, so the king decided to keep it a secret. He asked his wife and children to take turns to check the statues of the tortoises every day. But the queen reminded everyone that the beggarwoman had assured her that this catastrophe would not take place till the prince turned fourteen. The king thought about it but, for the sake of precaution, decided to start right away.

The two unmarried daughters were asked to take up the task of strolling across the palace and checking the tortoises' eyes every day. This way, nobody would be suspicious. And thus, the daily evening walks began. The two princesses and their staff would amble through the gardens every evening and walk to the palace gates. They would then stand at the gates to look at the local bazaar, throwing a cursory glance at the statues of the tortoises in the process. This continued for almost a year, and then the king, upon the insistence of the queen, decided to get both his daughters married, in case the great flood really did come.

The prince turned fourteen, and the responsibility of the daily inspection fell on him, since his sisters no longer lived in the palace. But the young prince found it odd to stroll in the gardens. *It's so unmanly*, he thought to himself. Instead, he decided to go to the local bazaar right outside the palace every evening and meet his subjects, asking after them and getting to know them better. This continued for some time, and he became good friends with the local butcher's son, who used to come to the market with his father to sell meat. The butcher's son was talkative and mischievous, and he got along well with the prince. They would meet every evening and exchange the daily goings-on. The butcher's son would tell the prince all the day's gossip, and the prince talked about the affairs of the palace.

One hot and humid summer evening, the butcher's son asked, 'Why do you come out to this dirt and noise every day? If I were you, I would just stay inside the palace and get my staff to find out about the city.'

The prince, being both naive and talkative, revealed the real reason. 'Well, since we're friends now, I will share my secret with you, but don't tell anyone. I don't come here for myself. It's for my father that I come every day.' He went on to narrate the story of the tortoises.

The butcher's son broke into a fit of laughter; he thought the king was foolish to believe the monk, who must just have been in a hurry to leave. 'How could a stone statue cry? And even if it were to cry, how could its tears be red? Tears are transparent, like the rain,' remarked the butcher's son.

'Well, that's what I thought, but my parents think otherwise, and I have to obey them. Maybe you can come to the palace some day after your work and look around.' Saying so, the prince went back to his palace, feeling a bit embarrassed. The butcher's son's eyes lit up with mischief, as the thought of red tears came to him. The next day, on his way to the shop, he collected some blood from a slab of fresh meat, sneaked to the palace gates and painted the eyes of the tortoises with it, making it trickle down their faces. He then quietly slipped back to his father's shop.

As usual, the prince left the palace that evening to speak to his subjects. When he saw the tears of blood falling from the tortoises' eyes, he was stunned. He could not believe what he saw, and he ran back to the palace to inform his father. 'Both the tortoises' eyes are filled with blood, and they have red tears rolling down their faces. It has happened, Father!' the prince exclaimed.

The king tried to calm him down. He summoned his wife and his prime minister, asking them not to tell the people anything, for it would cause panic, but to start preparing to migrate, just like the Great Monk had done.

Outside the palace gates, the butcher's son had been keeping watch all day, for he did not want to miss the prince's expression. He had seen the prince's face drain of colour when he noticed the bleeding statues. The butcher's son had rolled around with laughter, and then run to the palace to tell the prince that it was only a joke. But he was stopped by the guards at the gates and not allowed to enter.

Meanwhile, everyone at the palace was prepared to leave, and the king announced to his people what the Great Monk had predicted. Officers walked through the kingdom declaring, 'A great flood is upon us, and all of us must leave here at the break of dawn tomorrow with whatever belongings we can collect. The king will take care of the rest.'

The butcher's son heard the king's announcement and told his father about the prank he'd played on the prince. News of the prank spread, and some people decided to stay back in the city, including the butcher and his son. At sunrise the next day, the king left the kingdom along with the people who had decided to join the royal family.

A day passed, then two and then more, but no flood, no rain and no signs of impending doom could be seen. The people who stayed back rejoiced and congratulated each other for remaining in the kingdom. Some even raided the palace, taking whatever belongings had been left behind by the royal family. The king and his entourage, on the other hand, kept climbing to higher reaches, constantly looking back at the palace from their vantage points. After a few days of no rain, some, tired from climbing and the lack of proper shelter, decided to go back to their homes. The king, however, continued to climb upwards, in search of somewhere safe, never forgetting to provide food and bedding to his people.

On the ninth day after the blood sighting, it happened. The sky first turned ashen, then inky black. Hours of fierce thunder and lightning ripped through the heavens. The king's entourage took shelter under a giant rock and huddled together. They watched the city from there. Everything was covered in mist, and after a loud crash, it rained and it rained and it rained. On the eleventh day, some swear that they saw clouds burst above the palace and a chunk of the huge mountain slip down and crash into the palace, washing away the entire city and clearing all signs of existence, leaving a large lake where

the kingdom once stood. The rain kept falling, unabated, till everything became a blur.

On the fourteenth day, five days after disaster first struck, a rainbow appeared, arching over the ruins of the palace. A huge valley was created across the Yarlung Tsangpo river, which some say is right where the lake was created. This land slowly became so green and fertile that the king and his people, who'd come to settle there, soon became more prosperous than ever before. Those who had chosen to stay with the king thrived in this new realm.

In a few years, as the king grew old, he handed over the reins of his kingdom to his son, and retired with his wife to lead a monastic life. As he journeyed across the mountains, he turned around to take one last look at his beautiful kingdom. It looked lush and verdant, green as far as the eye could see. The king wistfully recalled the Great Monk's words: 'You've been kind to your people and to the monks, so you will find greener pastures beyond the flood.'

Several versions of this folk tale from Tibet are found in Bhutan, China and even Korea. Some think it is based on the Great Flood of China. Lions or dragons often replace the tortoises. In some interpretations, the Great Monk lives in the court of the king, or it's the royal daughters, and not the son, who reveal the family secret to the butcher's son.

Several folklorists have used this tale as an example of real events, such as the flood in this instance, being documented through lore.

Kesha Chandra and Gurumapa

Nepal

Kesha Chandra had always been a happy-go-lucky man. He had never cared about anything that was around him — he barely cared about himself. As long as he got his meals and some merriment, Kesha Chandra would not bother himself with worrying about the world. And Kesha Chandra really didn't have the worries that most people were vexed with. He didn't have to worry about earning a salary, because Kesha Chandra's father had left him a lot of money and a flourishing farm that was looked after by a battery of faithful helpers. Kesha Chandra didn't have to worry about cleaning his house, cooking or washing, because his mother had left him loyal attendants who took care of everything. Kesha Chandra didn't have to worry about making a name for himself, because his illustrious family had left him a famous surname. So, Kesha Chandra did what he liked. He loafed around during the day, gabbing away with the other idlers in the village, and gambled in the village club through the night.

Kesha Chandra also happened to be a handsome young man. He had a square face with a jawline that was the envy of many princes and kings. He had beautiful tanned skin and deep-brown droopy eyes. He had flowing brown hair and stood five feet and four inches above the ground, taller than most people around him. His chiselled body and broad chest gave him the air of a man of royal lineage, someone who had always lived in regal splendour and comfort. Kesha Chandra had everything that a young man his age could desire. But the one thing he lacked was a good friend who could advise him wisely and fairly. He needed a friend who would scold him when he was wrong and steer him away from wasting his life and fortune. But Kesha Chandra remained surrounded by men who just wanted to have a good time. These men liked Kesha Chandra for his money because his fortune would buy them everything they could not otherwise afford. Their greed pushed Kesha Chandra into bad habits. Left to himself, he would have whiled away his time playing the flute, like most hill boys and farmers do. But Kesha Chandra was never left alone by his useless friends. Slowly, he gambled away all his money, and nothing was left in his reserves. All the money that his father, grandfather and great-grandfather had left Kesha Chandra was lost in the gambling den. One night, when Kesha Chandra ran out of cash, he bet his palatial house in a game of cards. A few nights after he had lost his house, he bet all his farms and gold. He lost everything. Kesha Chandra came out of the club feeling lost, fearful and alone. He wasn't a bad guy, but he had been led astray by people with wicked intentions.

Left with no home, Kesha Chandra had nowhere to go. He was alone on the streets and was too embarrassed to ask anyone in the village for help. The village elders had warned him about his friends, and they'd urged him to stop gambling. But Kesha Chandra had never heard them out. Today, he regretted it. Since Kesha Chandra didn't want to humiliate himself further by sleeping on the road or in the village square, he decided to go to his sister's house, a couple of villages away. He had not even thought of her since her wedding two years ago, but he was left with no other option. It took him all night and some part of the day to reach his sister's village on foot. She was delighted to see her brother, but it also worried her because her brother had never visited her before. She wondered if bad news was to follow such an urgent, immediate visit. And her fears were not unfounded. She looked at her brother's face and knew something was wrong.

'Why do you look so tired, brother? And where is your buggy?' she asked.

Kesha Chandra offered no explanation but just said, 'Will you not offer me food? I have come to your house for the first time.' His sister felt guilty and rushed to the kitchen to cook his favourite dishes. She served him his meal on a plate made of gold. Kesha Chandra was famished and finished it all in no time.

When he was done eating, he noticed the plate was made of gold. *If I take this plate away and use it to gamble on my lost wealth, maybe I'll win everything back. After all, I have known how to play cards for ages. How could it go wrong?* he thought.

When his sister went back into the kitchen to douse the fire, Kesha Chandra quickly picked up the plate and called out, 'Sister, I have to leave. I am in a hurry. I'll see you later.'

His sister shouted, 'Wait, brother, I'm coming out.' But by the time she stepped out of the kitchen, Kesha Chandra and the plate were both gone. She noticed the missing plate and felt bad that her own brother had cheated her. But she did not say a word about it to her husband or anyone else in the family, for fear of bringing further disrepute to her brother.

Later that evening, when Kesha Chandra reached his village, his gambler friends noticed the big gold plate and immediately flocked to him. Kesha Chandra, though initially upset with them for abandoning him the night before, felt more confident with them on his side and began to gamble. But it barely took any time for Kesha Chandra to lose the plate. He was back to being a pauper. No sooner had he become penniless than his friends left him once again, telling him that they had to go back to their houses, but not before convincing him to borrow some money from his rich brother-in-law and sister. How else would he win back all that he had lost? Kesha Chandra wasn't sure if he could borrow from his sister, but since that seemed to be his only option, he began another trek back to his sister's village.

This time, Kesha Chandra's sister wasn't very pleased to see her brother. He understood that his sister was angry and could not muster enough courage to ask her for money. He was hoping that his sister would take pity on him and offer some money herself. Instead, she offered him food. Reluctantly, Kesha Chandra sat down to eat. This time, she served him food on a plate made of brass. Though not as expensive as gold, even brass, Kesha Chandra thought, would be valuable enough to make another go at winning his wealth back.

So, right after lunch, when his sister walked away to get some dessert for Kesha Chandra, he quickly picked up the plate and called out, 'Sister, I have to leave. I am in a hurry. I'll see you later.'

She shouted, 'Wait, brother, I'm coming out.' But just like before, by the time she stepped out of the kitchen, Kesha Chandra and the plate were both gone.

Kesha Chandra headed straight to the village club and showed his friends the brass plate. Even though his friends were disappointed that Kesha Chandra had not got any money from his sister, they were pleased with the plate and thought that it would be enough to get them an evening of revelry. Kesha Chandra and his companions gambled the night away, but it resulted in the same misfortune as always. Kesha Chandra's winning streak had ended many months ago and never returned. And once again, his friends deserted him. Left alone in the dark outside the club, Kesha Chandra felt a sense of panic. He had not just lost all his belongings but also the two plates that he had stolen from his sister's house. All in the hope of winning a game of cards.

Feeling immensely alone in his failure, Kesha Chandra could think of no one but his sister to turn to. So, once again, he began the trek to his sister's village and arrived there the next day at noon. His sister saw her brother and knew he had come back to get something valuable from her. She did not ask him why he looked so harried. Instead, she asked him to wash up so that she could feed him. Though he was slightly hurt, Kesha Chandra did not complain—he knew he was at fault. When he sat down to eat, his sister brought out all the food and kept it aside. Then she washed the floor in front of Kesha Chandra and served him all his favourite dishes right there on the floor. Kesha Chandra felt his stomach burn with humiliation. As soon as his sister went into the kitchen to bring back more food, he pulled out his handkerchief, tied up his whole meal in it and left his sister's house without saying goodbye. Kesha Chandra had never felt so disgraced. He had always found respect from his sister, and to be served food on the floor was the worst insult that had ever been thrown at him.

Distressed and degraded, Kesha Chandra started walking towards Swayambhu Forest, which was on Swayambhu Hill, also known as Gupuchha. The snub from his sister had cut so deeply into his heart that Kesha was lost in grief. He didn't keep track of how far into the forest he had walked. He trudged for days on end without stopping for even a minute. It was only after ten days that Kesha Chandra stopped. When he finally did, Kesha Chandra had walked deep into the forest and was far, far away from any sign of civilization. He had no strength left to go on. He fell to the ground, completely exhausted, and looked around. Tall trees, wild shrubs and undergrowth surrounded him. Kesha Chandra looked at the little bundle of food that he had been carrying from his sister's house. *I should eat this or else I'll die*, he thought. So far, as penance for his sins, Kesha Chandra had resisted eating the food. But now he felt faint and feeble. Kesha Chandra spotted a huge rock quite close to him, so he decided to climb it. Once perched there, he opened up his parcel to eat, but to his dismay, mould had grown all over the food, and it could not be eaten. Heartbroken by his misfortune, Kesha Chandra started crying. All he could do now was dry his food in the sun and hope that it would become edible.

As Kesha Chandra waited for the food to dry, he fell asleep. Seeing Kesha Chandra sleep, a flock of pigeons sitting on a nearby tree were tempted by the food. They flew down to the rock and ate it all up.

A few hours later, Kesha Chandra woke up from his nap and saw the food gone. He began to sob bitterly. His cries were heard by the king of the pigeons, who had his nest on the tree right next to the big boulder. The king was disturbed to see this young man looking so miserable. He flew to Kesha Chandra and asked him, 'What makes you cry so much, friend?'

Kesha Chandra narrated everything that had happened to him. Thinking of the day's disappointments tired him, and when he dozed off, the bird flew away. The king pigeon understood that it was his flock that had eaten all of Kesha Chandra's food. He called the birds to his nest and chided them for eating the man's food, and ordered them to lay droppings of gold on the boulder. The flock immediately set off to the rock to obey their king. Together, they laid a whole lot of droppings, all made of gold. When Kesha Chandra woke up from his nap, he found an enormous amount of gold around him.

Kesha Chandra was astounded. He rubbed his eyes hard to check if he was actually awake. He could barely believe it. He quickly spread out his muffler and started placing the gold on it, but the muffler was too small to hold everything, and the little he had gathered made the muffler too heavy to pick up.

As Kesha Chandra was struggling with the gold, he felt the ground below him tremble. Afraid that it might be an earthquake, Kesha Chandra sat down to gain his composure. He didn't want to fall from the boulder and hurt himself. The tremor was soon followed by a deafening growl. 'This must be my lucky day! I've found my breakfast in you. How handsome and strapping you are!'

Kesha Chandra wheeled around and was stunned to see a demon four times his size standing behind him. It was Gurumapa. He was a fearsome monster, who made the earth tremble when he walked, as well as the people on it.

Kesha Chandra had to think quickly to escape Gurumapa's clutches, so he blurted out 'Gurumapa, how wonderful to see you here! In fact, I came to this forest looking for you, as I wanted to invite you to my house.'

'Your house?' asked Gurumapa. This was a first for him. No one had ever invited him home before. People were terrified of him and ran away to safety at the mere mention of his name. 'Are you okay with me coming to your house?'

Kesha Chandra replied, 'Of course I am. There is no one stronger than you in this entire region. No one as powerful as you. I wanted to invite you to my house for a meal to tell you how much I respect you. How does one buffalo, two chickens and a cauldron full of rice sound to you?'

Gurumapa could not believe what he was hearing. He squinted at Kesha Chandra and said, 'Are you sure of what you're saying? You aren't playing a trick on me to escape becoming my breakfast?'

'No, no, no, Gurumapa! I wouldn't dream of playing a trick on someone as tough as you. I'm telling you the truth,' insisted Kesha Chandra.

But Gurumapa's rumbling stomach reminded him of his ravenousness. 'I don't care about your buffalo. I am hungry now and I am going to eat you. Now!' bellowed Gurumapa.

Kesha Chandra sighed and said, 'Okay, if that's what you want. I had come here to invite you for just one meal, but when I saw you for the first time, I was so impressed with how tall and broad you are that I had decided to keep you as a permanent guest in my house and feed you one buffalo, two chickens and a cauldron full of rice for every meal. It's such a pity that you want to eat me for just one meal and then go around looking for food. I wanted to take care of you for life.'

Gurumapa hadn't considered this at all. The offer seemed intriguing, and maybe too good to be true. He said, 'Are you sure you will be able to keep your promise if I come with you?'

'Yes, I am,' said Kesha Chandra, 'but on the condition that you will never eat me or anyone close to me. If you agree to this, come along to my house and I shall forever serve you.'

Gurumapa agreed. It was an offer no demon would ever refuse. Kesha Chandra breathed a sigh of relief. Now he could use Gurumapa's strength and big arms to carry all his gold for him. He told Gurumapa, 'You must help me carry this load. I had brought it for you as an offering. Now that you are going to live with me, you don't need it. I should take this back to spend on your comfort.' Gurumapa quietly picked up the heavy bundle, put Kesha Chandra on his shoulders and began his walk back to the village.

Their arrival brought much commotion. Kesha Chandra's friends queued up to gawk at the demon. When they approached Kesha Chandra, Gurumapa instinctively knew that these friends were freeloaders and shooed them away, threatening to gobble them up if they ever came close to Kesha Chandra. Meanwhile, the elders in the village welcomed Kesha Chandra and asked him about his well-being. They had been concerned about him ever since his disappearance. An old friend of Kesha Chandra's father even brought him food for the night and offered him his home to stay in. Kesha Chandra was moved by this outpouring of love, and he started to recognize who his well-wishers were. He promised to use the wealth he had found for the betterment of the village and its residents.

Over the next few weeks, Kesha Chandra built a beautiful palace-like house for himself on the outskirts of the village. He even sent pots of gold and brassware to his sister's house, along with precious jewellery and fine silks. He started spending time and money on the needs of the other villagers, and he was the first to offer help to anyone who needed it. All this while, Gurumapa lived in a huge barn right next to Kesha Chandra's house. Kesha Chandra kept his promise to Gurumapa, and sent him one buffalo, two chickens and a cauldron full of rice whenever he wanted a meal. After each feast, the demon would take an entire week to digest his food, sleeping for a whole day and night at a stretch after eating. It was always a week after his nap that he would ask Kesha Chandra for the same spread again. In return for the delicious food, Gurumapa would guard Kesha Chandra's house and keep his rogue friends at bay.

Time passed and Gurumapa began to accompany Kesha Chandra on his walks around the village. Children would scream at the sight of Gurumapa, and seeing this, their mothers started threatening them with tales of Gurumapa every time they misbehaved. On one of his visits to the village, Gurumapa heard a mother tell her son, 'Finish your meal or I'll call Gurumapa to take you away!'

When her son still refused to eat, she threatened him by calling out, 'Gurumapa, take this boy away. He doesn't listen to his mother. Take him away!'

Gurumapa, who always believed everything he heard or was told, thought that the mother actually wanted him to take away the child. Seeing that the child hadn't finished his food despite being told to do so, Gurumapa sneaked out of the barn that night, lumbered past the tiny houses and hoisted the child out of his bed. The missing child caused a huge ruckus in the village the next morning, though no one suspected Gurumapa of taking away the child.

A few weeks later, Gurumapa went back to the village with Kesha Chandra and heard another mother tell her daughter, 'Look, Gurumapa is here. If you don't listen to me now, I'm telling Gurumapa to take you away.'

Gurumapa smiled and made a mental note of the house. Again, that night he sneaked out of the barn to snatch up the little girl. And again, the villagers gathered to find the missing girl the next morning. They did not find any trace of her but also did not suspect Gurumapa of the theft because they had no reason to do so. Gurumapa had never been violent around them and seemed docile and harmless. They thought he was just a gentle giant.

Slowly, 'Gurumapa is coming!' started being regularly used as a threat for disobedient children, and every time Gurumapa heard such a threat, a child would go missing in the village, never to be found again.

However, Gurumapa's secret was soon revealed. An old man in the village had been intrigued by the number of children that were regularly disappearing. He started investigating the matter on his own, sleeping during the day to stay up all night and keep watch over the village after sundown. One night, when he was sitting atop a tree, he spotted Gurumapa sneaking into the village and devouring a child. The next day, he told the whole village about what he had seen. They banded together and marched to Kesha Chandra's house to tell him about Gurumapa's misdeeds.

The old man said to Kesha Chandra, 'I've seen it with my own eyes, so there is no scope for doubt. You must send Gurumapa away to the forest. He isn't fit to stay with us.'

A little old woman added, 'We cannot have our children become meals for Gurumapa.'

A young mother who had lost her child to Gurumapa wailed, 'This demon has to go. He has eaten my son and so many others. Kesha Chandra, you have to send him away.'

Under pressure from the villagers, Kesha Chandra had no choice but to send Gurumapa back to the forests of Swayambhu. Frustrated, he said to the demon, 'I can't help you, Gurumapa. Why did you take away all those children?'

Gurumapa innocently replied, 'But those parents wanted me to take away their children. You ask them! Every time I went to the village with you, they would tell their children that I would take them away. I only did what they wanted.'

Kesha Chandra was dismayed to hear Gurumapa's words. He pitied him for believing what the villagers had said. 'Oh, Gurumapa! They didn't mean it. Humans often use hollow threats to get their work done. This was a hollow threat too,' he said.

Gurumapa was taken aback by this deceit and said, 'How could I know that you humans say one thing and mean another? It's not fair.'

Kesha Chandra shook his head and replied, 'If only you had consulted me. Now I have no choice but to send you away.'

Gurumapa protested, 'I like being with you. I don't want to go away!' But nothing could be done. That night, the two slept uneasily, unhappy about how things had panned out. Kesha Chandra had been protected from his deceitful friends by Gurumapa all this time. And Gurumapa had loved Kesha Chandra for the care he offered him. Neither wanted to be away from the other, but they knew the villagers would have none of it.

The next morning, Kesha Chandra woke up early and went to the barn. Gurumapa was already up, worried about his fate. Kesha Chandra declared, 'I've got a plan.

You don't have to go back to Swayambhu Forest. I've been thinking all night and have found a place for you to live in peace. I'll still send you one buffalo, two chickens and a cauldron full of rice for your meals. I'll also visit you as often as I can.'

But Gurumapa wasn't interested and insisted, 'I am not going anywhere. I want to be here with you.'

Kesha Chandra implored, 'Look, Gurumapa. The villagers won't let you stay here. They'll push you out or even kill you if I insist on keeping you here. The best way out is if I shift you to a place close by but far enough from the village. You have to promise me not to return to the village ever again.' He paused for a moment, holding back his tears, and then added, 'But I give you my word that once a year, the villagers will hold a feast for you. As long as this village remains, its residents will bring you a gigantic feast on one special day every year.'

The thought of a feast brought a glint of happiness to Gurumapa's eyes. Kesha Chandra noticed this and whispered to Gurumapa, 'And do you know what the gigantic feast will be? Five buffaloes, 100 kilograms of rice, two gigantic cauldrons of black lentils and more than ninety other dishes, all village delicacies.'

For the second time since they had met, Kesha Chandra had made Gurumapa an offer he could not refuse. So, together, Kesha Chandra and Gurumapa walked to an empty plot of land, covered with grass, on the eastern side of the village. This area was known as Tundikhel. Kesha Chandra found Gurumapa a big tree in the centre of the field, called *chakla sima*. He built a makeshift house for Gurumapa on the branches of this tree and returned to the village after promising to look after the demon's needs.

Kesha Chandra kept sending food to Tundikhel. But one day, his assistants brought back an urgent message. 'Gurumapa did not touch his food. He said he wants to meet you and won't eat till you go see him.' Realizing the gravity of the situation, Kesha Chandra promptly left for Tundikhel.

Kesha Chandra was stunned when he arrived at Tundikhel. Gurumapa had wreaked havoc. He had turned himself into a wild bush and was sweeping across the ground like a powerful gust of wind. Grass, pebbles, twigs, leaves and rocks whirled around him.

Kesha Chandra was terrified. He ran to Gurumapa, pleading, 'Stop! Please stop, Gurumapa! What has happened? Why are you angry? Don't do this!'

Gurumapa heard Kesha Chandra's voice, paused and said, 'Oh, Kesha Chandra, so nice to see you. The thing is, I'm so bored. So, so bored. Why don't you take me back to the village with you? I have nothing to do here. Please take me back.' Gurumapa had not realized that while he was busy creating a tornado, a few children had brought their grazing cattle to Tundikhel. The children and the cows had all been swept away by Gurumapa's force, unknown to both Kesha Chandra and Gurumapa.

Kesha Chandra was sad to see Gurumapa's despair. But he knew he could not take him back to the village. He looked around to see if there was anything Gurumapa could keep himself busy with. His gaze rested on a pile of three stones. Quite close to that pile was another pile of three stones. And close to that one, another. There were many piles, some large, some small, but all made up of three stones. Instantly, he had an idea. He told the giant, 'Gurumapa, I know what can keep you from getting bored. Do you see that pile of three stones? From today onwards, you must do this for me—any time you find a pile of three stones in Tundikhel, you must separate them. Okay?'

Gurumapa looked around, saw a few piles and thought that this task would be fun. *When I'm done separating these rocks, I'll leave for Kesha Chandra's house, because there will be nothing more to do here*, he thought. He agreed to complete this job, and Kesha Chandra travelled back to the village.

For a few days, there was absolute calm both in the village and Tundikhel. Gurumapa was busy separating all the trios of stones and rocks, while the villagers carried on with their lives. But soon, the villagers began to worry about the children who had taken their cattle to graze. They should have been back home, but there was no sign of them or the cattle. The villagers gathered to figure out what could be done to find the boys. At the meeting, most people in the village agreed that it must be Gurumapa who took the children away again.

This time, they decided to teach him a lesson. A rogue friend of Kesha Chandra's, who had been shooed away by Gurumapa many times, had been waiting for an opportunity to get revenge. Hearing the villagers' cries of dismay, he jumped up and said, 'The only way to teach Gurumapa a lesson is to kill him. Let's go.'

Most of the villagers did not want to kill Gurumapa, but when they saw Kesha Chandra's good-for-nothing friends marching to the ground shouting, 'Kill him! Kill him!' there was little they could do to stop them. Meanwhile, Kesha Chandra was unaware of the goings-on in the village.

At Tundikhel, Gurumapa had just gone to sleep after separating piles of rocks all day long. He did not hear the villagers come. He did not even smell them, so tired was he from the day's work. He only realized that the villagers were agitated when they pulled him down from the tree and began to pummel him. 'What has happened to you all? Why are you hitting me?' cried Gurumapa, but the villagers were in no mood to listen. They kept landing blow after blow on him.

But something about attacking Gurumapa was not quite right. Every time the villagers hit Gurumapa, he would get up and start walking again, as if he had felt nothing. After all, Gurumapa was known for his strength and power, and it was not easy to defeat him. Kesha Chandra's wicked friend who had provoked the villagers was aware that a fight with Gurumapa would prove costly if the demon didn't die. Neither Gurumapa nor Kesha Chandra would spare him for his wickedness.

Noticing Gurumapa's strength, he shouted to the villagers, 'This won't kill him. There's only one way out. Let's unleash our horses on him and have them batter him with their hooves. That is the only solution.'

The mob agreed, and their horses were let loose on Gurumapa. As the horses trampled Gurumapa, his wails and howls of pain filled the air. The horses galloped through Tundikhel, wildly trampling everything under their heavy hooves, till they had no more energy to do so. No villager actually saw if Gurumapa had been killed, since the racing of the horses had created a dust storm around them. But when the cries of Gurumapa could not be heard any more, the villagers assumed that the demon had been killed. They then returned to their homes, satisfied that their children would never be harmed again.

Those in the know, however, believe that Gurumapa wasn't killed in the attack that night. He was dismayed at the hatred of the villagers and decided to disappear under cover of the dust storm, back to the Swayambhu Forest.

And for those who do not believe in the tale of Gurumapa and Kesha Chandra, wise old men have just this to say: 'Try putting a pile of three stones anywhere in Tundikhel at night. By morning, Gurumapa would have done his job.' Legend has it that the stones will always be found separated and neatly kept aside. For Gurumapa, they say, is still at work. Maybe he always will be.

This fable from Nepal is based on the myth of Gurumapa, a demon that is said to have tormented the people of Kathmandu a long time ago. Tundikhel, where the story ends, is a landmark in Kathmandu, used now for parades and concerts. Several festivals and rituals are still held in Tundikhel to mark the riddance of the demon. An annual festival of horse racing, called Ghode Jatra, is organized in memory of the horses that galloped through Tundikhel that night. What also remains is the gigantic feast that Kesha Chandra had promised Gurumapa when he urged him to leave the village. So, on the evening of a full moon night during Holi, the villagers have a procession and feast for Gurumapa. The feast is left in the open ground of Tundikhel, and people believe that Gurumapa devours the food once everyone has left.

But it's not just Gurumapa who is still remembered. Kesha Chandra is worshipped as a heroic ancestor, who could turn adversity into opportunity. In Nepal, Kesha Chandra's image is found on ancient scroll paintings and plaques that illustrate the legend of Gurumapa.

Rongnyu and Rongeet

Sikkim

Rongnyu and Rongeet had secretly been in love for a very long time. Away from the prying eyes of local inhabitants, the two would meet up in dark forests, behind huge boulders at the base of snow-clad mountains or in secluded meadows. If they were humans, Rongnyu and Rongeet would have spoken to their parents and found a way to get married. But the two were born rivers, young and unbridled, bursting with life and energy. In Sikkim, where they flowed, people believed that Rongnyu and Rongeet had been created by Goddess Eitbumo, who had also created all the animals, mountains, lakes, plants, stones and humans who lived on earth. They also believed that Eitbumo had always made her creations in pairs— never alone—so that everyone and everything would go through life with a partner to love and cherish.

Rongnyu and Rongeet had fallen in love the very first time they saw each other. And how could they not? It was all part of Goddess Eitbumo's plan. Rongnyu would often tell Rongeet, 'I feel this immense happiness when I am with you. I wouldn't leave your side for anything, unless you so decide.'

Rongeet's love for Rongnyu was just as deep, and he would say, 'Rongnyu, I would never abandon you, because with you I feel a sense of completion. How could I live without you?'

The two lovers kept meeting in private, till one evening, when Rongeet was on his way to meet his lady-love, he overheard some shrubs mocking him. They sniggered and gossiped that though Rongeet was young and handsome, he had become a worthless layabout, all because of ordinary Rongnyu. He heard them say, 'She has nothing special about her. Yet he's been bitten by the love bug.'

Rongeet was pained to hear this. While all was going well between him and Rongnyu, outsiders were a constant cause of worry for the two. Rongeet was tormented by the thought that others didn't accept their relationship. His fear wasn't entirely unfounded, because Rongnyu had to bear taunts from her friends too. No one thought it was respectable for two youngsters to be in love and meet secretly. Matches had to be made by families. When the two met the next day, Rongeet said, 'I think we should run away. That's the only way to live together.'

'Run away? Is that the right thing to do?' asked Rongnyu.

'We have no choice. Look at the jeers we get from the world around us. I don't think we can continue meeting like this. We have to run away.'

'But where would we go?'

'Down to the lowlands. In the forests. No one will recognize us there and no one will object.'

'Are you sure, Rongeet? I've never been there. Have you?'

'No, I haven't. But I know that it'll be safer for us.'

Rongnyu began to panic. 'Do you know how to get there? I have no idea at all.'

'Neither do I. But don't worry, Rongnyu. I will figure that out. I promise to take care of you and protect you.'

'We can go to the lowlands together, right?' pleaded Rongnyu.

'No, Rongnyu, we can't. Everyone will be suspicious if they see us leave together. We must travel separately.'

That evening, Rongnyu and Rongeet bade each other goodbye, with the promise of starting from their homes at dawn and meeting at the lowlands later that day. Rongeet's words kept echoing in Rongnyu's ears: 'Don't worry. I'll be there before you to receive you. I won't ever let you feel lost.'

Though the two lovers had decided to elope to the lowlands, they were clueless about how to get there. And how could they have known? Rongnyu and Rongeet had never left their homes. Concerned that they might lose their way, the couple resolved to seek help from someone who knew the way. So, after leaving Rongnyu, Rongeet went up to a bird and said, 'I have an urgent matter awaiting me in the lowlands. Would you be kind enough to guide me there?'

The bird, Tootpho, wasn't sure why Rongeet was asking her for guidance, but told him what she knew. 'It's straight down. Start from here and don't stop till you reach the plains—that's it. But why do you ask me for help?'

'Because you're the fastest creature there is. You fly swiftly and will face no obstacle, so I can watch you from below and follow you. I'm in a rush to get there, you see,' responded Rongeet. Tootpho nodded in agreement, and they parted, deciding to start their journey at daybreak.

Meanwhile, Rongnyu was worried about reaching the lowlands by herself. She had never travelled anywhere, let alone by herself. Rongnyu thought hard about who would be able to help her reach the lowlands, and was suddenly reminded of the serpent, Parilbu. She went to his house and earnestly asked, 'I have an urgent situation to attend to in the lowlands tomorrow. I've never been there and I'm not sure how I will make it without your help. Could you please help me?' Parilbu agreed.

The next morning, both Rongnyu and Rongeet left their homes with their guides. Rongeet raged down the mountain, following Tootpho, but balked to see the bird perch herself on a treetop, seemingly to rest. He had no choice but to wait for Tootpho to start flying again, losing a lot of time while he did. A little while after she began to fly again, Tootpho took a sudden detour.

Rongeet called out, 'Where are you going? You had said we have to go straight down to the plains. Why this detour?'

'Oh, I'll only take a few minutes. I've spotted some delicious fruit over here, and I'm starving. I can't fly on an empty stomach.' To Rongeet's dismay, these breaks occurred often, since Tootpho would either veer off course in search of food or stop to rest whenever she thought her wings needed a break. There was no ordering her to stick to business. After all, she was a bird, free to fly at will.

Meanwhile, Rongnyu was being led by the serpent. He wasn't as fast as Tootpho but was far more persistent. He didn't take any breaks and kept moving ahead, with Rongnyu quietly following him. Once at the lowlands, Rongnyu looked around for Rongeet, but he was nowhere to be seen. She began to worry that Rongeet may have lost his way, leaving her stranded by herself. After a few hours went by and Rongeet had still not turned up, Rongnyu thought it best to go back. She was just about to

leave in search of Rongeet, when she saw him forcefully rushing down the slopes.

Rongeet was surprised to see that Rongnyu had already reached. '*Thheesutha?*' he called out when he saw her. 'When did you arrive?'

Rongeet was upset with himself for not being able to keep his word to Rongnyu. He was so angry about not having been there to receive her, that he turned around and began to retrace his path without saying anything else to her. Rongnyu was puzzled. She didn't understand what had happened to Rongeet. She called after him, but he wouldn't listen. His ego was bruised, and he wanted to get away from Rongnyu, for she reminded him of his failure to get to the lowlands before her. As he raced back, he lost all sense of where he was going. He raged up the plains and the hills, and through the meadows, destroying everything that came in his way. His unchecked fury caused havoc. Looking at his rabid current, Rongnyu panicked. She raced along the same path that Rongeet had taken, hoping to calm him down. What she didn't realize was that her turbulent chase was adding to the damage Rongeet had already caused.

Rongeet and Rongnyu's furious flow resulted in a deluge, with all of Sikkim getting flooded. From animals to people to trees, everything started getting submerged. Only those who managed to perch themselves on higher ground were saved—most of them being the ones who rushed to Tungdon Lho, now known as Tendong Hill, which ended up being the only dry patch in the great flood. Desperate to be saved, the people of Sikkim started praying to Goddess Eitbumo.

'Nothing will be left of us or our homes if you don't do something. Save us, Mother Goddess.' Those who had been seeking refuge on top of Tungdon Lho fell to their knees. 'We know this deluge is a sign of your anger, Mother. Forgive us and save us, please.'

Eitbumo, who had been watching this devastation, said, 'You had forgotten me all this time, but since you have sought my help, I shall save your lives.' So Eitbumo transformed herself into a pigeon and landed on Tendong Hill. There, she picked up some millet with her beak and, turning towards the Kanchenjunga peaks, tossed some of it upwards, in an effort to placate Rongeet and halt his destruction. Some say that while the pigeon was throwing the millet, a few grains fell on her chest, which is why many pigeons still sport white spots on their bodies, right below their necks.

As soon as she had flung the millet, Eitbumo thundered, 'Stop, Rongeet, stop! Look at what you've done. This destruction is all because of you. Stop before your ego destroys even more.'

Rongeet heard Eitbumo's command and slowed down. She continued, 'Why are you angry? Just because you lost the way due to your guide and couldn't receive Rongnyu? Is that why? Or is it because you came second and Rongnyu came first?'

Suddenly, things were put into perspective for Rongeet. He stopped in his tracks. *Why* am *I angry? Why can't I accept that Rongnyu arrived before me? Is it really my bloated ego that is causing me such pain?* he thought.

Realizing his mistake, Rongeet felt regretful and ashamed of the destruction he had caused in Sikkim. He begged, 'Please pardon me, Mother Goddess. Pardon me. I have been a fool, consumed by my ego. I did not realize what I was doing. I have caused you, Rongnyu and the people here immense harm. Please forgive me.'

Rongnyu, who was listening to all this, hastened towards Rongeet. She was overcome with guilt for adding to the chaos that Rongeet had unleashed, and was hurt to see Rongeet's remorse and disgrace. She hugged him tightly and said, 'It's not your fault, Rongeet. You were misled.'

Rongeet embraced Rongnyu, and together both of them turned to Eitbumo. 'Mother Goddess, can you pardon us? Please show us mercy.'

Eitbumo saw how shamefaced the couple was, and blessed the two with eternal love and companionship, saying, 'May you always be together and always be in love.'

Rongeet turned to Rongnyu and promised, 'I shall never fail you like this again. And I won't ever lose my cool. I know that you are always by my side.' Hand in hand, Rongnyu and Rongeet moved back towards the lowlands. When they arrived, they merged into each other, transforming themselves into one waterbody, and started flowing down the plains, never to be separated again.

Even today, they say that the water of the rivers can be seen as two different bodies, up until they meet. Those who visit the confluence of Rongnyu and Rongeet have come back with tales of two differently coloured rivers flowing over each other. It's nothing short of amazing: the river splits into two, light green on top and dark brown underneath. Some believe that since the great flood, Rongeet has never left Rongnyu's side, and he flows above her to protect and look after her.

In Sikkim, it's common for newly married couples to visit the confluence of Rongnyu and Rongeet, to seek blessings from the two river bodies in order to have an eternally blissful married life.

This folk tale comes from the region of Sikkim, or Mayellyang as it was earlier called, and is the most popular Lepcha folk tale. The members of the Lepcha tribe are said to be the children of the surrounding snowy peaks and were created by Goddess Eitbumo. Many of them make a pilgrimage to Tendong Hill to pray to Goddess Eitbumo and offer fermented millet beer to Rongeet, in order to placate his anger and seek his blessings.

Rongeet's cry of 'Thheesutha' got distorted through the years, finally becoming 'Teesta'. It is believed that the spot where Rongeet met Rongnyu became the point of emergence for the Teesta river.

Lakshi, Dulal and the Monkeys

North Bengal

Lakshi and her husband, Dulal, had been together for many years. Though they had been set up by their parents, and their two tribal communities had come together to celebrate the union, Lakshi's cousins had dragged her to the village fair to catch a glimpse of Dulal before their wedding. Between giggles and mischievous stolen glances, Lakshi had told her cousins that she liked Dulal and would be happy to be with him for the rest of her life.

Since their wedding day, Lakshi had devoted herself to Dulal and his family. She had moved into Dulal's small hut, which was in a huge compound shared by his relatives and separated from the neighbours by a low stone wall, and she quickly adjusted to the ways of his family.

A few years later, Dulal's father passed away, followed rather swiftly by Dulal's mother. The family had been struck by tragedy twice within one year. The last few months of Dulal's mother's life had been particularly taxing because of her desire to see Dulal and Lakshi's children. 'I want to play with my grandchildren,' she would tell her son. Often during her sickness, she would urge her daughter-in-law to do something, but there was little Lakshi could do to help. Dulal's mother passed away with this unfulfilled wish in her heart.

After the demise of her in-laws, Lakshi was left all alone in the house, with no one to look after or even talk to. In order to fill her days with some activity, she started accompanying Dulal to the fields to help him with the work there. As time passed, Dulal and Lakshi realized that they wouldn't be able to have children. Instead of cursing their luck, the two decided to put their hearts into something else. They began to take care of the animals around their house. They would tend to the stray dogs and cats in their neighbourhood. On their way to the fields, they would stop to feed the squirrels and birds. They would even offer their hay to the stray cows. Everybody in the village respected the couple for their empathy and compassion.

One year, the village experienced a terrible summer. Temperatures rose every day. First, all the plants wilted, and then the ponds and wells dried up. Before the villagers could come up with a solution to the unbearable heat, the blazing sun set alight the forest on top of the hill. The inferno raged for several days, and the woodland animals fled in search of shelter, many of them singeing and maiming themselves in the process. The villagers took turns to guard their livestock from the fire and from runaway leopards that were hunting for food. For two days and two nights, the villagers dug a deep trench between the forest and the village, filling it with water. This, they hoped, would keep the fire from spreading to the village.

When their situation hadn't improved, the villagers turned to God. Like all the others in the village, Lakshi and Dulal went to the ancient shrine of their tribal god to seek divine intervention. 'Try offering a sacrifice to the lords every day. Give them what is dearest to you all. It will help appease them,' the priest suggested to everyone. So, the village folk took turns to surrender their most precious items. But the fire raged on.

One day, when Lakshi and Dulal were cutting the dried stock in their fields to feed the cattle in the village, they spotted a baby monkey, lying crumpled on the ground. Lakshi rushed to him and offered him some water in a bowl. The monkey could barely sit up, so Dulal helped him with the bowl. The monkey drank thirstily. He sat up only for a moment and immediately collapsed again. Lakshi took pity on him and gave him some of the nuts she had carried for their lunch. The monkey picked up a few nuts and slipped them into his mouth. Even before he had swallowed them, he picked up another handful. He was ravenous, so Lakshi offered him all that she had packed from home. The baby monkey looked like he had been hungry for days. He finished Lakshi's ration for two all by himself. He then drank some more water and climbed the nearest tree to rest. Lakshi and Dulal, though hungry, found satisfaction in the fact that a starving baby had been fed. On their way back, all Lakshi could think of was the poor baby monkey. How had he saved himself from the forest fire? 'The poor baby must have lost his mother in the fire. He must be so heartbroken. Perhaps he trekked a long distance in search of food and water. Maybe we should have brought him back with us. What if some bigger animals attack him?' Lakshi said to her husband.

Dulal, who believed in destiny, assured Lakshi that if God had taken care of the monkey so far, he would take care of it further as well. 'After all, he looks after all his children, doesn't he?' he told Lakshi.

That night, the rain gods relented, and it rained. There wasn't enough to soak the dry earth, but the light shower permeated the soil deeply enough for the beautiful smell of wet mud to surface. Lakshi heard the pitter-patter of droplets on the roof. She shook awake her husband and pulled him to the courtyard, where all their relatives had gathered to celebrate the rain. Lakshi, filled with joy, whispered to her husband, 'It's because of the baby monkey! If we hadn't helped him, this village would have remained cursed.' Dulal's soft smile confirmed that he felt the same way.

The next day, the sun was bright and harsh again. It seemed impossible to believe that the previous night had seen any rain at all. Lakshi and Dulal packed some nuts and bread, and they headed for the fields again. This was going to be another usual day unless Lakshi could find the baby monkey. She had thought of him all night. As the two made their way through the village, Lakshi's steps were quick, her gait brisk. She wasn't waiting to talk to her neighbours about the previous night's showers, which was the only thing anybody was discussing. Each household seemed to have a different reason for why it had rained. One family was sure that the rain had come because the village head had sacrificed his rare gems. Another insisted that it was due to the five days of fasting by the village's oldest woman. Yet another said, 'It's the death of that ominous owl! It had been hooting for days. Its passing has rid the village of the bad omen.' Lakshi overheard these comments as she hurried through the village, but she was sure that it was her baby monkey that had brought the rain.

As soon as Lakshi got to the field, she frantically looked for the monkey, but it was nowhere to be found. She was disappointed and worried. What if a bigger animal had killed it? Her mind started racing, and she could not get herself to work after that. Understanding her grief, Dulal consoled her, saying, 'He was just a monkey, Lakshi, and monkeys never stay in one place. He must have gone away, looking for food.' Lakshi knew that there was some truth in what Dulal was saying, so with a heavy heart, she started to work again. After a few hours, as the sun turned towards the west, clouds gathered around and hid it in their folds. The fields were enveloped in darkness. Both Lakshi and Dulal looked up to check where the sun had gone. Suddenly, they heard some squeaking from the trees. Lakshi jumped with joy, for what she saw was priceless. A troop of monkeys, swinging from tree to tree, was making their way into Lakshi and Dulal's field! At that very moment, droplets of water began to fall on Lakshi's and Dulal's faces. Their eyes darted from the clouds above to the swaying monkeys. A trickle of joy ran through their hearts, just as a sprinkle of rain fell from the heavens.

This time it didn't just rain, it poured. It poured like the skies had opened up completely. Nothing could hold back the water. The sky turned grey, thunder boomed and lightning, sharp and dazzling, ripped across the mountains. Lakshi and Dulal's happiness knew no bounds. They did a little dance in the rain, celebrating the downpour. The dry, parched land was soon soaking wet. The rain was falling so hard that Lakshi and Dulal had to seek shelter under the barn on the edge of their field. They couldn't walk back home in this deluge. Once the rain stopped, Lakshi offered all the nuts she had to the monkeys, who had been sheltering in the shed adjacent to the barn. The monkeys filled their mouths and happily ate all they could. Lakshi was thrilled to see the little baby monkey she had fed the day before. Now, he was being protected by the older monkeys and was well taken care of. Once the nuts had been eaten, the monkeys returned to the forest, and the couple returned to their village. Lakshi was joyous, for she had hope that she would see the baby monkey and his clan again. Perhaps the next day. And the next. And the next!

The rain gods must have been listening when Lakshi made her secret wish to see the monkeys again. They became regular visitors to the couple's farm. As time went by, Lakshi and Dulal started taking care of the monkeys like they were their own children. Every day, when they went to the fields, they would get food for the monkeys to eat. The monkeys would arrive at a chosen hour and eat in the field. They wouldn't bother Lakshi and Dulal but would get up to some mischief that would leave Lakshi and Dulal's neighbours furious. After all, monkeys are naughty by nature and often more destructive than other creatures. True to their habits, the monkeys would do something or the other to inconvenience the neighbouring farmers. If one day they would destroy all the fruits on a tree, the next day they would pluck flowers and scatter them on the ground. This annoyed the other farmers, and they would run after the monkeys with sticks and stones, ready to punish the mischievous lot. Lakshi and Dulal had to intervene each time to protect the monkeys. The villagers constantly complained and urged the couple to stop feeding them, as they were now becoming a nuisance.

Lakshi and Dulal often had to hear the villagers taunt them, many even hurling curses at the couple. But they were helpless. They had no children of their own, and over the years, these monkeys had become family to them. They were to Lakshi and Dulal what children are to parents, so the worst of their mischief found little anger from the couple. It wasn't that they didn't see

that the monkeys were annoying the other farmers. It bothered them that the monkeys would ruin the crop of their neighbours. In fact, while feeding the monkeys, Lakshi would often talk to them, telling them to abandon their destructive ways. But monkeys are monkeys, and they couldn't give up mischief. As time passed, Lakshi and Dulal grew old, but the group of monkeys stayed on with them, approaching the couple every day for food.

One season, the couple decided to sow sweet potatoes in their field. They were both growing old, and they knew that they wouldn't be able to work for much longer. Sweet potatoes would bring in more money, and if the couple grew enough, they would get by without having to work for two seasons. They decided to put all their savings into buying sweet potatoes to sow, so that they could have a good harvest. In the wholesale market, the previous season had seen a very high price for sweet potatoes. It was expected to be even higher this year. Of course, the stakes were high too, and a large investment had to be made, which meant taking a big risk. The couple decided to take their chance and leave the rest to God. If their gamble paid off, the crop would fetch them enough to live comfortably for a while, after which they hoped to rent their field to younger families who could give them a portion of the crop, as well as the annual rent. That, the couple thought, would be good enough to see them through their old age.

On the day that the sweet potatoes were to be sown, the couple set out very early, starting work in the field before daybreak. The previous weeks had been spent ploughing the field and getting the land ready for sowing. This morning, the couple dug equidistant holes that were deep enough to sow the potatoes into the field.

By afternoon, they had planted the potatoes and were ready to water the soil, when the monkeys arrived.

Lakshi laid out the nuts and bananas for them and the monkeys gorged on the food. The eldest of the lot spotted a leftover sweet potato and ate it. It was so delicious that he asked Lakshi for more. Lakshi shook her head and said, 'There's none left. We've planted all of them. I have nuts and bananas for you. Why do you ask for sweet potatoes?'

The monkey was disappointed to hear that and argued, 'Lakshi, sowing the potatoes just as they are will not give you a good yield. Don't you know the ancient method of sowing sweet potatoes that is far better?'

Lakshi was all ears now. She urged the monkey to tell her what this technique was. The monkey responded, 'If you had boiled the sweet potatoes, wrapped them in banana leaves and then sowed them, then the yield would have been much better. The potatoes would even have a hint of banana.' The couple consulted each other and agreed to follow the formula the monkeys had just spelt out. They dug up the potatoes and took them back to their hut. That evening, Lakshi boiled all the sweet potatoes, and Dulal neatly wrapped them in banana leaves. The next day, they went back to the field and sowed them in the holes they had dug earlier. They were exhausted from the sowing they had done the day before, and having to do it all over again drained them completely. As they sat down to rest by the tree, the monkeys came to the field. Seeing them approach, Lakshi got up to serve them food. But the monkeys had other plans. They told Lakshi and Dulal to go home and rest, offering to water the field for them. They didn't need Lakshi to serve them. Surprised that the monkeys were insisting on helping them, the couple wondered what had changed for the monkeys to suddenly be so kind. But their weak bones and frail bodies could not say no to the help being offered to them.

So, happy that the monkeys could help them, the couple returned home.

Sadly, the monkeys weren't really being kind. They had a different plan and were only thinking of how they could get hold of some boiled sweet potatoes, their favourite food. They could have stolen the raw potatoes that had been planted the day before, but Lakshi and Dulal's boiled potatoes would be even better. No sooner had the couple left than the monkeys dug up the field, took out all the potatoes and started eating them. What they could not eat, they threw away. The people working in the neighbouring fields saw this, and two of them ran to the village to inform Lakshi and Dulal. The others just stood along the edge of the farm, looking at the destruction the monkeys were causing. They did not stop the monkeys, because they thought that Lakshi and Dulal would finally learn their lesson. All these years, the villagers had been telling the two that while the monkeys treated the couple well, they wreaked havoc in other people's lives and fields. But the couple doted on the monkeys and would not pay heed. By the time the couple arrived, their entire field was ruined, and the sweet potatoes were either eaten or destroyed. The two slumped to the ground as they saw their entire life's savings destroyed. There were neither tears nor anger; there was only a hollow sense of despair. They sat hunched in the corner until it got dark and the last of the neighbouring labourers urged them to get back to the village. Lakshi was too stunned to say anything. She had not expected to be cheated by the monkeys. Dulal was starting to get angry. His savings were gone, the sweet potatoes were ruined and he felt completely stupid for trusting the monkeys. He decided to teach the monkeys a lesson. He now understood what the other villagers had been going through. That night, Dulal plotted to punish the monkeys and told his wife about it. Lakshi, though not keen, could not oppose Dulal, for she feared his anger. The next day, Lakshi and Dulal got to the field an hour before the monkeys usually did. Dulal walked into the barn and lay still on the floor. Lakshi sat outside. As soon as she spotted the monkeys, as tutored by Dulal, Lakshi began to wail. Hearing her loud howls, the monkeys approached her and asked her what was wrong. Lakshi told them that when Dulal arrived at the field in the morning and saw the destruction there, the shock was so huge that he fell unconscious and may not have survived. 'I've been trying to revive him for the past half hour, but he hasn't moved an inch or spoken a single word,' she cried.

The monkeys peeped inside and saw Dulal lying motionless in the centre of the barn. Though some were worried, a few of them were relieved, as Dulal's illness meant that no one would punish them for their villainy the day before. The monkeys wandered around, while Lakshi continued to bawl. She paid no attention to the monkeys. In fact, she did not even offer them any food. Feeling sheepish and not sure how to approach Lakshi, the monkeys decided to send their youngest member over to her. When the young monkey pulled Lakshi's finger again and again, asking for food, she pointed to the barn and said, 'Food's there. I can't lay it out for you. Go get it yourself.' She added, 'There are also some sweet potatoes left over from yesterday.' The monkeys jumped up at the mention of sweet potatoes and raced to the barn.

Following the troop, Lakshi quickly closed the door as soon as the last monkey went in. Once the monkeys were all inside and busy eating the nuts and sweet potatoes, Dulal got up quietly and tiptoed out of the barn. He turned around, locked the door from the outside and called out to the monkeys from there. 'You menacing monkeys, look here!' Dulal thundered. Startled to hear Dulal, the monkeys abandoned their food and looked around. There was no sign of the man. They rushed to the window and peered out. There Dulal was, standing in front of the window with a thick stick in his hand. On seeing the monkeys, he said, 'Now I will teach you a lesson. You destroyed my potatoes, my savings and my life. I've locked you inside and will leave you locked up for the rest of your lives. This is your punishment.'

The monkeys were puzzled and shocked. One of them dashed to the door and pulled at it.

'It really is locked!' he screamed.

The other monkeys were starting to panic. 'But you were unconscious. You were lying still on the ground,' said one to Dulal.

Another added, 'Weren't you unwell? Were you pretending this whole time?'

A third monkey, angry at being conned, yelled, 'You cheated us, Dulal! You cheated us. You rogue, you crook!'

Dulal let out a huge roaring laugh and repeated the words slowly. 'Cheat! Rogue! Crook! Look who's talking!'

The monkeys realized that Dulal was actually referring to them and their misconduct. Their greed for their favourite food had led them to cheat their greatest supporters and caregivers, Lakshi and Dulal. They looked at each other and their heads fell in shame.

Dulal wasn't done. 'My wife and I took care of you as if you were our own children. Even when we didn't have food for ourselves, we fed you all. Our neighbours complained about you, but we still cared for you. And this ruined field is what you give me in return?' he exploded.

Lakshi began to sob. Between muffled snivels, she said, 'I always treated you so well. Why did you do this?

If you had asked me for some potatoes, I would have given them to you. Why did you trick me? You have destroyed not only this field but also everything else. My trust, our love and our relationship. You killed it.' Inconsolable now, she ran towards her house in the village, and Dulal followed her. The monkeys remained where they were, punished for their behaviour.

For a while, the monkeys sat around, thinking that Dulal and Lakshi would come back to release them. They were thirsty and wanted to go to the well to drink some water. They were also itching to play in the trees, but there was no way out. The only window in the barn had firm wire mesh over it, so all they could do was look out of that.

As night fell and Lakshi and Dulal had still not come back, the monkeys became fearful. What if Dulal kept his promise and never let them out? What if the couple never returned to the field? What if they never managed to escape? Distressed and exhausted, the monkeys dozed off.

Back in the village, Lakshi and Dulal's neighbours were happy to hear about the punishment given to the monkeys. The villagers visited Lakshi and Dulal with food and gifts, as a mark of their gratitude for teaching the monkeys a lesson. Lakshi was sad to receive the gifts. To every guest who came to her house, she said, 'My children have been punished today. I can understand your sentiments, but I cannot accept your gift.' When Dulal tried comforting her, Lakshi said, 'I supported you when you wanted to punish the monkeys, but now that you have punished them, I should be allowed to grieve like a mother would.' Dulal was overcome by Lakshi's sense of justice and affection, and he asked her what should be done with the monkeys.

Lakshi urged him to release the monkeys, since keeping them locked up was of no use. 'Besides,' she said, 'they have learnt their lesson.'

Indeed, the monkeys were regretting what they had done. When they woke up in the morning, the oldest monkey spoke first. 'What we did to Lakshi and Dulal was simply awful. They took care of us for so many years, and we just got greedy and forgot all about their kindness. Greed always faces punishment. Greedy ones like us can never lead a happy life in the long run, and all of us trapped here, hungry and thirsty, are an example of that.'

One of the younger monkeys said, 'So we deserve to be locked up here. We shouldn't get a better life after what we did.'

Another monkey added, 'We should have paid kindness with kindness. This old couple has taken care of us for years. We thrived only because Lakshi gave us food every single day. What fools we have been.'

Meanwhile, Lakshi and Dulal were feeling awful for punishing the monkeys. They had always treated the monkeys like family and were sad that they had been so severe with them. It was particularly awful for Lakshi because she had always believed that many, many years ago, the village had found respite from the drought and heat due to the monkeys. In exchange for the food and care Lakshi had provided their little one, the monkeys had blessed the village and its residents. Lakshi was convinced that her kindness to the baby monkey had been reciprocated by kindness from the gods. To be cruel to the same set of monkeys today was heartbreaking for her. The villagers, however, were happy that the monkeys had been punished and were unable to harm anyone else. In their happiness, Lakshi and Dulal's neighbours offered them money to plant another batch of sweet potatoes and to help them look after their field.

When morning came, Lakshi and Dulal quickly put some food together and started for the farm. As they approached the field, Lakshi's heart sank at the sound of silence. She was worried that the monkeys were hurt. 'We shouldn't have locked them up. They must be hungry and in pain. They've never been imprisoned like this,' she told Dulal. He too was feeling remorse for his stern action against the monkeys. He chose to stay silent though, not reacting to Lakshi's words. Instead, he walked up to the door of the barn and yanked it open.

Inside, the monkeys were huddled in a corner, smaller monkeys piled on the larger ones, helpless and afraid. As soon as they saw Dulal, they jumped up, ran to him and cried, 'Forgive us, Dulal. We have been very mean to you. We didn't realize what we were doing. Forgive us, please!' Dulal couldn't hold his tears back any more and started to cry.

Just then, Lakshi caught up with him. She saw the monkeys, regretful of their mischief, and Dulal, regretful of his anger, and she thought it best to put an end to everything right then. She promptly fished out the nuts she had carried for the monkeys and laid them on the floor. 'I got you this. You must be hungry,' she said.

The oldest monkey, who had engineered the plan to steal the sweet potatoes, burst into sobs when he heard Lakshi, and wrapped his arms around her. 'Forgive us, kind soul. Forgive me, for I planned all the mischief. Forgive me, for God will never pardon what I did.'

Lakshi hugged the old monkey tightly and said, 'All is forgotten, old man, as long as you realize your mistake and feel repentance. God and I both forgive you because forgiveness brings love. Holding grudges doesn't. Now eat!'

That day, Lakshi fed the monkeys with her own hands, and Dulal joined her. The monkeys promised them that they would never harm any other farmer again. They blessed the couple with a bumper crop in return for their kindness. That year, Lakshi and Dulal produced the sweetest of potatoes, which were all picked up at a high price. They earned enough to save for their old age and even managed to rent their field to a newly-wed couple.

While Lakshi and Dulal never went back to work, the monkeys, as promised, stayed away from the fields in the village. They sometimes visited Lakshi and Dulal, and on those days, the couple would feed the monkeys and play with them like parents do with their children. Over the years, Lakshi and Dulal would look after other stray animals too, setting an example for their neighbours.

It is said that ever after, animals became an important part of every villager's life, and a special and unbreakable bond was established between humans and creatures. Even now, though mischievous, monkeys continue to inhabit human settlements and find food and love from people like Lakshi and Dulal. The love that Lakshi and Dulal had for animals has blossomed and flourished even after their time.

This tale is from the hills of northern Bengal. Different versions of the folk tale are found in Manipur and other north-eastern states, like Tripura, as well. In some versions, Lakshi and Dulal plant potatoes, *loklei* or arum instead of sweet potatoes. The story also has various dramatic endings. While in many the couple kills the monkeys in rage, others have a lone monkey that survives the wrath of the old couple and calls upon demons to punish Lakshi and Dulal.

Tejimola

Assam

One of its names, popular in Assam and specially amongst the Bodo people, is Burlung Buthur. The Tibetans, though, call it Yarlung Tsangpo, believing it originates on the Angsi Glacier on the northern side of the Himalayas in the Burang county of Tibet. In India, it is popularly known as the Brahmaputra, literally meaning the son of Lord Brahma, one of the lords of the trinity of Brahma, Vishnu and Mahesh. Whichever name it goes by, this vast river could easily be mistaken for a sea. Big ships and vessels sail up and down the river for trade, transport and fishing, and many villages dot its banks.

In one such village lived a small-time trader, along with his daughter, Tejimola, and his wife. Tejimola was the only child the couple had and was the apple of her parents' eye. Both of them loved everything about their daughter. Tejimola grew up to be an obedient and loving child, much to the delight of her parents. Before he would set out on his travels, Tejimola's father would ask, 'What does my baby Teji want this time? What will make Teji happy?' It was a ritual he never gave up, and he would always bring her something special from the places he'd visit. Tejimola's father was so fond of his daughter that he would fail to remember anything his wife might have asked him to bring, but he'd always bring whatever little Tejimola had asked for.

And Tejimola would ask for quaint, sometimes bizarre, gifts. She had little idea what her father would find in the strange, magical lands he would visit, and so she'd pull ideas from her imagination: dancing dolls, clips with white daisies on them, a skylark, a silver birdcage and pink water lilies, fresh as dew. Her doting father would move heaven and earth to fulfil her wishes.

Though the trader enjoyed travelling and knew his livelihood depended on his journeys, it broke his heart to leave his wife and child behind every time he left home. His travels were long and tiring, varying from a week to a few months, and this unpredictability often left him feeling lonely and homesick. He had attempted quitting his job, trying his hand at other types of work in the village: farming, running a grocery shop, fishing and moneylending. But he lost money in all of these businesses. Trading was the only job that remained profitable.

One particular monsoon, when the trader had left home for a month, Tejimola's mother fell sick. Her neighbours took her to the village healer, but she found no relief from his medicines. Her fever would rise every afternoon and dip in the evening. It made her writhe in pain. She would call out, 'Help me, Teji's father! Relieve me of this pain.' Her repeated calls for help saddened her relatives, and they tried to get in touch with Tejimola's father. But even days of repeatedly sending messages did not bring him home. He was somewhere so remote that the messages never reached him.

One afternoon, the sky turned blood red, and Tejimola's mother cried out, 'Save me, good lord. I cannot take this pain.' Tejimola, who had been playing in the courtyard, ran to her mother, as did her cousins. As she entered the room, young Teji saw her aunt lay down the limp body of her mother on the bed. Her mother was silent now and looked at peace. Tejimola was too little to understand what had happened, but she knew it was something terrible.

A storm raged that evening and night, like the world itself was coming to an end. Neighbours and relatives thronged the house, despite the downpour, to stay by Tejimola's mother's body, which had now been put on the floor. It rained the next day as well, and Tejimola heard people discussing if they should wait for her father.

One of the old neighbours said, 'We have sent a few urgent messages, so he should be coming soon. We should wait.'

Another man said, 'But what is the guarantee that he will come? We haven't heard from him so far.'

Another visitor added, 'We will have to make a decision by the afternoon. We can't let another evening go by without cremating the body.'

Cremation was a word that little Teji did not understand. In fact, she was so little that she didn't understand the concept of death or mortality. She didn't make much of the conversation and stayed in the corner of the room, playing with the adolescent girls who had accompanied their parents to her house, ignoring the rest of the crowd. Though her mother's stillness puzzled her, she had been told by most of her relatives over the previous weeks to leave her alone so that she could rest and get better. *Mother is so still. She's getting so much rest that she'll feel better really soon*, Teji thought.

Finally, as the afternoon aged and the rain began to ebb, the villagers decided that Tejimola's mother's last rites had to be done, even though her father wasn't home. As her family readied to take Tejimola's mother's body, a village boy came running into the house, crying, 'He's here! He's here!'

Tejimola turned to see who it was and ran to the door when she saw her father standing there, surrounded by a group of people who were holding his trunk and other belongings. The young girl wrapped herself around her father's knees. He scooped her off the ground and into his arms.

'Baba, where have you been? I missed you! What have you got me this time? Did you find the white lily I asked for?' Tejimola's questions were incessant and innocent. She was far removed from what had befallen her parents, one gone forever and the other shocked at what life had thrown at him. Tejimola's father looked at her sweet face and slumped to the ground. Grief was flooding his heart. Without looking at Tejimola, he picked her up again and walked to his wife's body. The sight of her lifeless body was too much to bear. He had never felt the need to openly express his love for his wife, but he had never imagined a life without her. She was the reason his life felt complete.

Tejimola kept pulling at her father's sleeve, asking, 'Baba, what has happened to Ma? She has been lying still like this for two days.' When he didn't respond, she repeated, 'Baba! Baba, listen. Look here. Answer me, Baba. Why aren't you talking to me?' She burst into sobs for the first time since her mother's passing away. Tejimola's voice and sobs seemed far away and while he wanted to reach out to her and console her, his own overpowering grief had made him unable to do that. He stood motionless, in a state of shock. The villagers saw how devastated he was and pulled him away from the body.

Days passed, and the trader stayed home with his daughter, spending all his time with her. Tejimola was thrilled to have her father around, since she had never got to spend so much time with him, but she remained lost without her mother. She repeatedly asked for her, and her father made one excuse after another. He didn't know how to explain her mother's death to her.

Tejimola would say, 'Baba, Ma should have been back from the river by now. She has taken too long. Should we go and check?' Tejimola's father didn't know what to say, for he had told his little girl that her mother had gone to the river with her friends. Before this, when Tejimola's father told her that her mother had gone to a relative's house to help out, Tejimola had protested, 'There's so much work to do here. Why doesn't she come back? She keeps going from one place to the other and doesn't think of us.' And, with an air of finality, she had concluded, 'Tell her to be back by the weekend. Otherwise, I will never speak to her again.' She was done with excuses now and wanted her mother back. He had been lying for a while, and didn't know how much longer he could hide the truth from his daughter.

The neighbours initially sent food, but after a month, all the household chores were left to the trader. Relatives had been taking turns to come home and look after Tejimola, consoling her father when they saw him. Each one of them had the same advice for Tejimola's father: 'Get married again so that you will have somebody to take care of Tejimola.' At first, he was very reluctant, but as time passed, the trader realized that he would have to go out to work and Tejimola would need someone to take care of her. Finally, Tejimola's father relented, and a *choti ma* was brought home for Tejimola.

Tejimola's stepmother was a young bride and a distant cousin of Tejimola's mother. Young Teji thought this new woman had been brought in to play with her, and she took to her instantly. Though Tejimola's stepmother initially enjoyed playing with her, she soon found her to be a bother. She was too young a woman to enjoy being a mother to a small child. But she could not reveal her true feelings for Tejimola, for she would be asked to leave the house immediately. So, the stepmother pretended to be very fond of her stepdaughter and was very nice to Tejimola when the trader was around. But when he was away, she would trouble the girl, for she had grown to hate Tejimola. Her distaste grew with every trip that the trader took. As he had always done, he would only ask Tejimola what she wanted him to bring back home for her from his travels. Just as he had done with his first wife, not once did he ask Tejimola's stepmother what she may have desired. His actions left a deep feeling of resentment in her heart.

If the trader had been fond of Tejimola before her mother's death, after her passing away, his love and attention for Tejimola was absolute. There was no room for anyone else in his heart. If even something tiny happened to Tejimola, the stepmother would be sharply scolded by the trader. It was no surprise then that as time passed, she began to hatch a plan to get rid of Tejimola.

One day, when the trader announced that he would be gone for a month-long business trip, Tejimola's stepmother decided that this was her chance to rid her home of the girl. By now, Tejimola was a beautiful young teenager. The night before the trader set sail, he told his wife that on his return, he would organize Tejimola's wedding to his distant cousin's son, who lived five villages away. He also told her that he had saved up for Tejimola's wedding all these years and would use all these savings for the occasion. He would be left with only his house.

As the would-be groom belonged to a rich family, there were certain expectations that had to be met.

'Tejimola is all I have. Whom have I earned so much money for? If Tejimola is taken care of, I'd retire a happy man,' he said to Teji's stepmother. 'The family is very nice, and my Tejimola would be happy there. My savings will ensure a good wedding. That's all they want—no dowry or anything. As for us, we can live well by selling vegetables,' he concluded.

Tejimola's stepmother was very upset to hear this. She had always prided herself on how rich her husband was. If all his wealth was about to go away with his daughter, she would become a pauper like everyone else. She was determined to not let that happen.

The next day, as the trader made his way to the river, the stepmother allowed Tejimola to attend her cousin's wedding in the village next to theirs. What was surprising was that her stepmother not only gave Tejimola permission to go when she had earlier refused to but also lent Tejimola her finest *mekhla*, a beautiful type of saree, to wear. Tejimola's stepmother had said to her, 'If there is anyone at that wedding that all eyes must be on, it has to be you, so you must wear my mekhla, the finest in the village.'

When Tejimola protested, her stepmother announced, 'If you won't wear my mekhla, I won't let you go to the wedding.' Tejimola was bewildered by this sudden act of kindness but didn't make too much of it. She quickly packed her bags with the mekhla inside and left for the wedding.

But the stepmother had a plan to trap Tejimola. She had hidden a small rat between the folds of the mekhla. When Tejimola reached her cousin's house and unpacked her clothes to get ready for the evening, she noticed a rat running out of the bag. When she opened up the mekhla, she felt a knot in the pit of her stomach, as she realized that the rat had eaten through the delicate fabric of the mekhla and had completely ruined it. Tejimola burst into tears, terrified of her stepmother's anger. Her cousins consoled her and offered her replacements to wear for the evening. But the fear of her stepmother did not leave Tejimola for even a second, not that evening at the wedding and not on her way home the next day.

As soon as Tejimola reached home, the polite, sweet stepmother of the day before was gone, as though she had never existed. In many ways, that was the truth. Without inquiring about the wedding or Tejimola's journey, the stepmother demanded that her mekhla be returned immediately, for she knew what must have happened. Tejimola began to sob. She fell at her stepmother's feet and cried inconsolably for forgiveness, explaining what had happened.

The stepmother was seething with anger. She dragged Tejimola to the barn, where the huge pestle and mortar used to grind rice was kept. She had planned this for days and was not going to miss this chance to punish Tejimola. The stepmother started to pound the rice and told Tejimola, 'Fill the mortar up with rice.'

As Tejimola began to add the rice, her stepmother started pounding faster and faster, crushing Tejimola's right hand in the utensil. Even as Tejimola yelled and squirmed in pain, the stepmother ordered, 'You nasty, irresponsible girl! Don't stop adding the rice.'

Tejimola pleaded, 'My hand is crushed. I'm bleeding. I'm in pain.'

Her stepmother did not relent. She commanded, 'Use your left hand. Do not stop. You ruined my mekhla. Now do as I say.' Tejimola had no choice and started adding the rice with her left hand. Her stepmother began to pound and crush Tejimola's left hand too.

Satisfied that both her hands had been mangled, the stepmother insisted that Tejimola use her legs to shove the rice into the mortar, and she pounded them to a pulp, and then battered Tejimola's head, killing her. The stepmother's anger had now waned. She was satisfied that Tejimola was dead and would not bother her or claim her husband's riches. While Tejimola had been at the wedding, her stepmother had dug a big hole in the backyard, where she intended to hide her stepdaughter's body. She buried Tejimola's body in the grave and planted a jackfruit tree on top of it. She decided to tell her husband that Tejimola had run away to attend her cousin's wedding and had never returned.

A few days passed. One afternoon, some passers-by called out to the stepmother, asking her for some jackfruits. The stepmother was surprised and responded, 'I have no jackfruit. Go away.'

The passers-by told her that the tree in her backyard was laden with jackfruits. 'You are such a miser. You wouldn't miss anything by giving us one jackfruit,' they said. The stepmother hadn't noticed, but in a matter of days, the jackfruit tree had magically grown to its full size and was laden with jackfruits.

Worried that they would start asking about Tejimola, she shouted out, 'Just take as many as you want.'

The passers-by ran to the tree and greedily started to pluck the low-hanging fruit. But just as they began to do so, they heard the fruits cry out, 'My name is Tejimola. My stepmother killed me by crushing my head, and she buried me under this tree. Please help me by telling my father that I am here.' The passers-by were shocked, and they left the tree and confronted Teji's stepmother, cursing her and telling her what they had heard. She shooed them away and ran to the backyard. She was shocked to see how tall and fruit-laden the tree was, and she brought out the axe, cut down the tree and threw all the fruits away in the front garden.

A couple of days later, Tejimola's stepmother once again heard the neighbours calling out to her, asking her for bitter gourd. The stepmother did not even bother stepping out of the house, and she shouted, 'Are you mad? Where do I have bitter gourd?'

When the villagers insisted that her front yard had a creeper loaded with bitter gourds, her eyes nearly popped out of her head. She was reminded of the jackfruit tree but was in a hurry to get rid of the neighbours, so she told them to take whatever they wanted. The bitter-gourd creeper had magically grown in the very place where Teji's stepmother had thrown the jackfruits. The neighbours started picking the fresh bitter gourds from the front yard, when they heard them cry, 'I am Tejimola. My stepmother killed me by crushing my head, and she buried me under the jackfruit tree. This bitter gourd has grown from the seeds of the jackfruits. Please help me by telling my father that I am here.' The neighbours were shocked and ran back to tell the stepmother what they had heard. They asked her where Tejimola was. The stepmother got rid of the neighbours by telling them that Tejimola was with her cousin. As soon as they left, the stepmother pulled out the entire creeper and threw it into the Brahmaputra river.

A few weeks later, Tejimola's father was returning from his travels, when he saw a beautiful water lily in the river. Though he was carrying numerous gifts for Tejimola's wedding, he remembered how much she loved water lilies and bent down to pluck it for her. When he touched the flower, it said, 'Father, I am your Tejimola. Stepmother killed me by crushing my head, and she buried me under the jackfruit tree. The seeds from the tree gave way to bitter gourd, and when thrown into the river, the bitter gourd turned into this water lily.'

Her father was shocked to hear Tejimola's voice, but he knew that the stepmother was capable of something evil. However, to be sure that this wasn't a witch or a trap, he took out some betel leaves, placed them on his hand and said, 'If I loved my daughter truly, my Tejimola will transform into a skylark and eat the betel leaves from my hand. Otherwise, this flower will drown in the water.' No sooner had the trader said so than a beautiful skylark rose from the waters, fluttering her wings, and perched herself on the trader's hand, pecking at the betel leaves. The trader quickly caught the skylark, coaxed her into the silver cage that he was bringing back for his daughter and rowed back to the village.

On his way back, the trader listened to the entire story from the skylark, and once he reached home, he asked the skylark to transform into his daughter, Tejimola. She did so, and on seeing Tejimola alive with her father, the stepmother knew that she had no future in the house. She ran out, screaming, 'Ghost! Ghost!' Her neighbours tried to stop her, telling her that there was no ghost around but only Tejimola and her father, who had come back together. But Tejimola's stepmother neither listened nor stopped.

She kept running till she escaped the village and its people, and she was never seen by them again.

A few months passed, and Tejimola's father wed her to the boy he had in mind, as planned. Tejimola's father gave up his constant travelling and instead started growing jackfruits in his backyard, bitter gourd in the

front garden and betel leaves in a patch near his house. By selling these, he made enough money to live a respectable life and did not return to the river for trade again.

In the villages along the Brahmaputra, skylarks are often seen calling out through the day and night. Sometimes, they break into a peculiar tune which local residents call the 'T Song'. They say that when the skylarks are singing this rare tune, they are telling the story of Tejimola. This tune might sound like any other melody to most, but those with a trained ear and an understanding of emotions can hear Tejimola's story in the haunting tune that the skylarks sing on the banks of the Brahmaputra.

The story of Tejimola, sometimes called Teji or Teja Teji, comes from Assam. This has remained one of the most popular folk tales in the state. Several discussions have been held to understand its popularity. Some say that parents like to tell this fable to their daughters to make them brave and to teach them to fight against all odds. The tale has several versions in the north-east and in Nepal as well. In some versions, Teji's deceased mother comes to help her, while others have an additional family member in the form of an evil stepsister.

Bumo Sing Sing Yangdonma

Bhutan

For four full hours after her father had left for their fields to look after the wheat and barley crop, Donma had been working at her backstrap loom. Her mornings were usually spent weaving because that's when she was alone at home with nothing needing her immediate attention. The afternoons would be spent cooking. Donma and her father had only each other for company. Her mother had passed away when she was a little girl, leaving her in the care of her father. Donma's father doted on his little angel and had always made sure that he attended to all her demands and needs. Together they lived in a small cottage in the Chume Valley.

Today, Donma was busy weaving a blue silk scarf for her father, with the intricate traditional Bhutanese designs that he liked so much. Donma wanted to give him the scarf on his birthday, which was a week from now. So, like every day, this morning too Donma was sitting in the back lawns of her house, weaving her yarn of love. Suddenly, something fell from the skies straight on to Donma's *kira*, a traditional ankle-length Bhutanese skirt. A black-necked crane flying past had dropped an unusual fruit in Donma's lap. She had never seen anything like it before. It was orangish-red in colour, smelled very sweet and was so temptingly fresh that Donma couldn't stop herself from eating it. As soon as she finished eating the fruit, she longed for more because it was unlike anything that Donma had ever had before. That evening, when Donma's father returned from the fields, she told him about the fruit that the crane had dropped and how she was craving to eat more of it.

After listening to the description of the fruit, Donma's father understood that the fruit was a special tangerine that grew in the orchards of the demon Meme Sinpo, who lived across the seven valleys. 'You can't eat that fruit, my child—it is of a rare variety,' said Donma's father.

'But I want more, Father! I just can't do without eating it. Please get me some.'

'I would, sweetheart, if I could. But this fruit grows in the orchard of the giant demon Meme Sinpo, who lives across the seven valleys, and you know we are forbidden to go there.'

But Donma would not listen. She started crying. She had set her heart on the fruit and would not rest till she ate some more of it. Donma's father couldn't see his daughter cry. In the years after his wife's death, Donma's father had tried his best to ensure Donma didn't ever have occasion to cry. Seeing her sob so bitterly broke his heart, and he agreed to go to the demon's orchard. As night fell, he filled a small bag with some essentials and a folded sack that he would use to bring back the fruit and started on his long journey.

For a month, Donma's father kept walking, crossing mountains, forests, rivers and valleys. A day after the month had passed, he reached the gates of Meme Sinpo's orchard. The evening sun was just setting on the horizon and Donma's father could see the giant demon walking in his fruit-laden garden. The red hue of the sunset bounced off Meme Sinpo's dark body, giving him an even more monstrous appearance. Meme Sinpo's huge size and periodic grunting echoing across the valley scared Donma's father. He crouched behind a bush and thought that he would wait for night to fall, for the demon to go inside his house, and then steal some fruit for his daughter. Once it was completely dark, he tiptoed into the orchard, climbed up a tree full of the tangerines and carefully but hurriedly started plucking the fruit and filling his sack. Once he was done, he climbed down the tree and started walking towards the gate of the orchard, happy that he had collected enough fruit for Donma and would soon be on his way home. But just as he was slipping out of the gate, his foot got caught in the fence and he fell on the ground with a loud thud.

Meme Sinpo, who usually slept inside his house, had today accidentally fallen asleep under a tree in his orchard. The sudden crash woke him up with a start and he looked at the gate. There, in the darkness, he saw a human lying on the ground. He raced towards the body and was surprised to see an old man with a sack full of tangerines looking at him.

'Who are you? What are you doing here with my fruit?' Meme Sinpo asked.

'I am no one—just a poor farmer who needed some fruit for my daughter.'

'So you stole my fruit? I will kill you for this. No human steals from my orchard!'

'I would have asked you if I had met you. Since I did not find you in the orchard, I just plucked a few tangerines,' muttered Donma's father.

'You liar! I am going to eat you because I know you stole from my orchard.'

Donma's father fell at Meme Sinpo's feet and started begging, 'Please! Please spare me. Don't kill me. I am the only parent my daughter has—she will be all alone without me. Spare me and I will do anything you want.'

'Anything?'

'Yes, anything. You can have everything I have—everything.'

'What do you have?'

'A cottage and some land.'

'I don't need that. What else do you have?'

'Nothing at all. My daughter and I are poor people.'

'But you do have a daughter! Ah, yes! Now, this is what I want—bring me your daughter and I shall leave you alone.'

'No! I can't bring you my daughter. She is my only child,' Donma's father protested.

'Okay then. Get ready to die.'

Donma's father was overcome with fear. If the demon ate him, Donma would be left alone. He couldn't bear to imagine that. He had to think of a way to save both Donma and himself from the demon. So he said to Meme Sinpo, 'I will give you my daughter only if you can discover her name.'

'That is simple. I can do this easily. You watch me now.'

With that agreement, Donma's father once again set off across the seven valleys. This time, though he was both worried and sad, he walked faster. He wanted to get to Donma as soon as he could. When he got home, he told Donma about his encounter with Meme Sinpo and warned her not to tell her name to any stranger that she might meet.

Back in the orchard, Meme Sinpo was desperate. He couldn't wait to lay his hands on this young girl from the Chume Valley. So he sent his favourite assistant, a pig, to Donma's house to find out her name. On arrival, the pig hid himself in a corner of the garden from where he could keep an eye on Donma and her father. For five days, the pig could make out nothing. On the sixth day, Donma's father came back from the field and did not find Donma in the kitchen as usual. He looked for Donma all over the house, but couldn't find her. Anguished that Donma may have been taken away by the demon, he started calling out, 'Bumo Sing Sing Yangdonma, where are you? Bumo Sing Sing Yangdonma, come to me! Bumo Sing Sing Yangdonma, are you in trouble? Bumo Sing Sing Yangdonma, answer me!'

'I am here!' screamed Donma from the back of the house.

Donma's father ran to the garden at the back of the house and saw her lying in a pit. 'How did you get there?' he asked.

Donma told him how she had been cooking in the kitchen when suddenly, she heard a noise in the garden. When she went to check, she accidentally slipped and fell into the pit. Unable to emerge from the pit, she lay there with a twisted ankle, waiting for her father to come home. She had expected him to look for her and find her there. Donma's father pulled her out and they went in. What they didn't see was that Meme Sinpo's assistant the pig had seen and heard all of this.

Quietly, he slipped out of the bush and started running to his master's house reciting 'Bumo Sing Sing Yangdonma' so that he didn't forget the name. When the pig was just one valley away from Meme Sinpo's house, he was tempted to stop and catch his breath, because a little way ahead, he spotted his favourite patch of grass where he had always enjoyed resting. *A few hours won't delay me unusually. Let me get some rest because once the master knows the name he will take me along the same distance again to bring the girl here*, he thought.

When the pig woke up, a good part of the day had gone. He had slept longer than he had anticipated. He shook himself awake and ran to Meme Sinpo's house. Sinpo was thrilled to see the pig and asked, 'Did you find out her name?'

The pig answered with equal excitement, 'I did, I did!'

'Tell me what it is!'

'It is . . .' The pig froze. He had forgotten the girl's name! While sleeping, he had forgotten to recite the girl's name over and over as he had during the journey. He looked at his master with deep regret and told him what had happened. Meme Sinpo was furious and did not even wait for the pig to apologize. In one swoop, he ate the pig and ordered his second assistant, the monkey, to go to Chume Valley and find out the girl's name.

The monkey reached Donma's cottage and hid himself in a tree. For a week, he sat there without any success. On the seventh day, Donma's father came back from the fields and was very upset to see Donma lying still on a cot on the porch. This was a first because on every other occasion, Donma would hear the slightest sound from her father's shoes and come running to the gate to meet him. He thought Donma had been attacked and succumbed to her injuries. In distress, he started wailing, 'Bumo Sing Sing Yangdonma, what happened to you? Bumo Sing Sing Yangdonma, wake up, child! Bumo Sing Sing Yangdonma, talk to me! Bumo Sing Sing Yangdonma, don't leave me!'

'Leave? Where am I going? I had just fallen asleep, Father. What is wrong with you?' said Donma, rubbing her eyes as her father's wailing woke her up.

Donma's father was relieved but the monkey was ecstatic. He had done what the pig could not do and started imagining the great number of bananas his master would offer him as a reward. He slipped out and swung from one tree to the other, chanting 'Bumo Sing Sing Yangdonma' throughout the journey to the demon's hilltop.

Right outside, in anticipation of the monkey's success, Meme Sinpo had collected a huge mound of golden bananas. Sinpo thought if the monkey came back with the name he would reward him with this mound of bananas. The monkey, hungry from his travels, thought, *The master brought these for me. If I eat a few bananas, he won't mind.* So he sat down to gulp down some of his favourite food. A little while later, when he met Sinpo and was asked about the name, like the pig, he couldn't remember a thing. Irritated with the monkey, he picked him up and ate him in one bite.

Next, Meme Sinpo sent his most trusted agent, the bee, to do his job. The bee flew to the Chume Valley and found herself a nice corner on Donma's windowsill. She stayed there for two days and on the third heard Donma sing to herself, 'Bumo Sing Sing Yangdonma is singing a song! She's wearing a pink dress! Bumo Sing Sing Yangdonma is plaiting her hair! She's wearing a dress in pink!'

The bee looked at the bright pink dress Donma was wearing and figured that she was singing about herself. She promptly got off Donma's window and started winging towards Sinpo's house. On the way she kept repeating, 'Bumo Sing Sing Yangdonma' so fast that it almost sounded like she was buzzing constantly. That day, unlike Meme Sinpo's previous assistants, the bee got back to her master and told him Donma's full name. Meme Sinpo's joy knew no bounds and he immediately left for Donma's house, flying there at top speed.

At the door, he called out to her father and said, 'I have come to take Bumo Sing Sing Yangdonma. Tell her to leave with me at once!' Donma's father was grief-stricken but he knew there was nothing he could do now. So Donma left her father's cottage and the Chume Valley on Meme Sinpo's back.

Sinpo and Donma travelled for five days and five nights through beautiful valleys and mountain ranges. Finally, Donma and Sinpo arrived at a rocky hilltop with a single dark and dingy house on it, surrounded by a huge orchard full of the tangerines. Donma was elated to see the fruits, thinking at least this would keep her happy during her stay here. Her father had lost all the fruit he had collected for her in his encounter with the demon. She got off the demon's back and reached out to pluck a ripe, orange tangerine, but the demon pulled her back and dragged her into the house. There, he put her in a wicker basket only big enough for her to sit in, and hung her upside down from the roof.

Bumo Sing Sing Yangdonma had never been treated like this. She did not expect the demon to be nice to her, but she hadn't expected him to imprison her in this beastly manner. Anguished, she started crying, only to be interrupted by Sinpo's sister, who had been told to keep an eye on Donma while Sinpo was catching up on his sleep. Sinpo's sister shouted, 'Crying won't help! The more you cry, the longer you will stay in that basket, hanging upside down.'

Donma was so dejected that she continued to sob. So Sinpo's sister called out louder this time, 'Stop crying.

My brother will keep you there longer if you cry. He doesn't want you to be happy.'

Suddenly, Donma muffled her sobs and asked, 'Your brother doesn't want me to be happy?'

'No, he doesn't. Because of you he lost two of his assistants. So he won't allow you any happiness here.'

That gave Donma an idea. She turned her head towards Sinpo's sister and started laughing loudly. Through the mesh of the wicker, she said, 'I am not crying. I am trying to muffle my laughter. I am so very happy here. I can see heaven from here and it is beautiful.' Sinpo's sister was astonished to hear this and asked, 'You can see heaven? Are you serious?'

'Dead serious. Do you think I could lie in this position?' 'I want to see heaven. What does it look like?' 'Can't explain, sister. It's just amazing! Out of this world!' Sinpo's sister was now both curious and jealous. She couldn't believe that Donma could see heaven from her basket when she had to merely stand around and guard her. She quickly hauled Donma down to the ground, got into the wicker basket, asked Donma to pull her to the roof and fasten the rope on the side so tight that nothing could bring her down. This was just what Donma had been waiting for. She tied Sinpo's sister up so tightly that even Sinpo would take time untangling her.

She then ran around to check the rest of the house and was astonished to see prisoners in Sinpo's house. One room was full of children, another full of women and yet another had young men caged inside. Donma unlocked all the doors and asked them to flee as fast as they could. As Donma was running out of the house, she saw a small door on the far-left corner of the main corridor. Uncertain if anyone was inside, Donma first thought she'd run away but then decided to peep in. What if there were more people trapped inside?

As Donma stepped into the room, she saw an extremely frail old lady sitting in a corner. She ran up to her and said, 'Run! We have very little time left — Meme Sinpo may wake up any time now.' The old woman looked at Donma, squinting to protect her eyes from the light that now filled the room through the open door. She said, 'I can't run, I am too old. You should run, or Sinpo will kill you.'

'But I must free you! You must be as old as my mother.'

The old woman smiled and told Donma, 'It's a waste of time to help me escape — I don't have the energy for it. But since you have called me mother, I shall tell you that I came here as Sinpo's young bride and once I grew old, Sinpo imprisoned me here. It is only a matter of time before he kills me. I want you to run away as fast as you can before Sinpo gets up.'

Donma didn't want to leave the old woman behind but she had little choice in the matter. As she was rushing out of the door, the old woman called her and said, 'Take this — I have no use for it now.' She then pulled off her old wrinkled skin, all the way from her feet to the thighs, abdomen, over the shoulder and then over her head. She handed it to Donma and said, 'This will be your ultimate disguise. Wear this and even Meme Sinpo won't be able to recognize you.'

Donma put on the skin as fast as she could and started running with all her strength. She ran non-stop for one hour. Once she thought she had covered enough distance, she sat down to catch her breath. She had barely been sitting for ten minutes when she heard the loud growls of Meme Sinpo. Donma froze and thought her time had come. She raised her hand to cover her face and instead saw an old wrinkled finger. Suddenly, she remembered that she no longer looked like herself and was safe from Sinpo. She turned her back to Sinpo and sat patiently. As Sinpo approached Donma, he grunted, 'You, old woman! Have you seen Bumo Sing Sing Yangdonma anywhere?'

Donma pretended she couldn't hear and said, 'Speak louder. Can't hear you. I am old.'

Sinpo was angry and blared, 'Have you seen a young woman running past?'

Donma shook her head and said, 'No, not here.'

Sinpo became more agitated and started running towards the Chume Valley, calling out, 'Sing Sing! Sing Sing!'

Donma sat there for a while, waiting for Meme Sinpo to cover some distance to make her escape easy. As she waited, two young men came up. They were carrying long bamboo sticks on their backs. When the first one came close to Donma, he yelled, 'Move out of my way, old woman, or these bamboos will hit you.'

Unperturbed, Donma said, 'Jump over me if you like or step off the road. I can't move — I am too old.'

The young man, frustrated by Donma's answer, jumped over her. No sooner had the first man passed than the second man came by. This time without waiting to be asked, Donma said, 'Jump over me or step off the road — the choice is yours.'

The man looked at Donma and decided to step off the road. As he did that, the bamboos hit Donma's back, and the young man stopped to apologize. His kindness did not go unnoticed and Donma thanked him for it.

Once the men were gone, Donma picked herself up and started to walk on. A little distance away, she saw a lake and was tempted to drink some water. But to drink water, Donma needed to peel off the old woman's skin. She looked around to see if there was anyone watching, and with no one in sight, she started taking off the old woman's skin.

Just then, the second young man returned. He was regretting hitting the old woman and wanted to offer her some food. When he saw Donma taking off the old woman's skin, he was perplexed. He walked up to her and asked, 'What are you doing? Is this some kind of magic?'

Surprised by the man's presence, Donma broke down and told him her entire story. The young man looked at Donma closely and was mesmerized by her beauty and innocence. He bent down and told her, 'I am captivated by your beauty, but more than that I am dazzled by your bravery. I am the prince of the Tang Valley and have been sent here by my father to complete a test. Would you do me the honour of being my wife?'

Donma was stunned and didn't know what to say. She barely managed to utter, 'You will have to ask my father. We live in a small cottage in the Chume Valley.'

That afternoon, the prince and Donma set off to her house to seek her father's permission for marriage. Donma's father couldn't have found his daughter a better husband and agreed to the match instantly. For ever after, Bumo Sing Sing Yangdonma lived happily with her prince in his massive castle. Meme Sinpo, they say, is still exploring the Chume Valley looking for Donma. Ever so often in the valley, one can hear him growl and hiss with the wind, his voice echoing 'Sing Sing! Sing Sing!'

This is one of the most popular children's tales in Bhutan. It is sometimes called the Sing Sing Yangdolma story. Different versions of the story exist in various parts of Bhutan. Some elders believe that bees make their buzzing sound due to chanting Sing Sing' for their master, Meme Sinpo, all the way from Donma's house to his. The story also encourages young girls to use their strengths to fight evil and script their own destinies.

Many Bhutanese people will recall it as being the first folk tale they heard from their grandparents.

The Flying Monks

Arunachal Pradesh

For 400 days, Master Ekaijinko had used different techniques to build patience in his 100-odd pupils. These were novice monks who had come to stay in the Urgelling monastery of Arunachal Pradesh. Master Ekaijinko was to train them in the Lamaistic Mahayana school of thought. Surrounded by the Himalayas and the Tawang Chu Valley, the monastery had been established in the fifteenth century and lay a few kilometres to the south of the town of Tawang. Urgelling, with its beautiful setting in the higher reaches of Arunachal Pradesh, was considered the perfect place for young monks to build their patience. The snow-capped Himalayas surrounding the monastery not only provided an awesome view but also served as a reminder of man's insignificance and microscopic size on Earth.

Master Ekaijinko's pupils, though, were a peculiar lot, and despite over a year of meditation, had found little reserves of patience within themselves. One day, as Master Ekaijinko was holding a special session on ego and fear in the prayer hall, a bee entered the room. The students slowly began to move as the bee flew closer to them. Master Ekaijinko sensed that his sermon was being overshadowed by the buzz of the bee. He opened his eyes and saw some of his students attempting to dodge the bee, while others tried to swat it. Master Ekaijinko was ashamed of the lack of endurance in his students. His teachings had made little impact on them. He dismissed the class, telling his students that he was going to the meditation room and must not be disturbed while there.

After six days of non-stop meditation, Master Ekaijinko came out of his room. His stubble had given way to a slight beard, but he looked peaceful and strangely happy. His students were puzzled by their master, for every time one of them came close to him, all he would say was, 'Go away.'

Unable to understand what their master wanted, a student called Bankei asked, 'Master, what do you want us to do? We can't understand your words, even though they must be full of wisdom.'

Master Ekaijinko asked Bankei to gather all the pupils in the prayer room, for he had a special announcement to make. Once in the prayer hall, Master Ekaijinko said to his students, 'I seem to have failed you and myself every day of the last year. Seven days ago, I realized that I am a good monk, but I may not be a good teacher. As your master, I ask you to retreat to the higher reaches of Mount Gorichen, the house of the Kameng river.' His students gasped—Gorichen was the third-highest peak in their region. Master Ekaijinko added, 'I want you to climb to Gorichen and come back only after you have mastered your thoughts. Remember, mastering your thoughts does not mean that you should not think at all. It means you should be able to absorb what you see, learn something from that and then control what you are thinking.'

At daybreak the next morning, Master Ekaijinko saw his disciples leave one by one. He had forbidden them from carrying any belongings, reminding them that controlling their thoughts required hard-earned patience. The students had listened to their master in silence, but most of them had found his instructions harsh and bereft of any sympathy. This, however, was their fate till they achieved what their master wanted them to. As the last of the students walked out of the gates, Master Ekaijinko, standing tall on the roof of the monastery, called out, 'Do not stop till you reach the top of the mountain. Observe and absorb everything on the way. Every solution will come from that.'

Master Ekaijinko's students walked non-stop for weeks, making their way through thick vegetation, crossing small brooks and bigger ponds, dodging herds of cattle that rushed at them and protecting themselves from bad weather. Many of the monks were still concerned about food, looking for berries they could eat, since they had nothing to eat with them. The others were more concerned about what their fellow travellers would scavenge, as they were depending on them to find a meal. Their master's instruction to observe and absorb was lost in this search, and it was clear that little had been learnt when the students reached the top of Mount Gorichen to meditate. In the year that they had spent at the monastery, the students had learnt to meditate but not internalize much. So, when they arrived at the summit, they sat down to do what they had practised for so long but hadn't yet learnt. They crossed their legs in the lotus position, mindfully breathing in and out, until their hunger proved stronger than their willpower.

Three weeks into their meditation, the students were overcome by ravenousness. They decided to abandon their task and return to the monastery. As they were walking down, the students came across a reed-thin man. Despite his lean frame, he looked strong. The man had a large deer slung over one shoulder. Clearly, he was returning from a hunt. The deer was so big that it seemed impossible that the hunter had killed it by himself and carried it all the way up the hill.

The hunter looked at the monks and asked, 'Where are so many of you young monks going together?'

One of the monks replied, 'Back to our monastery.'

'Oh! To Urgelling, is it? Ekaijinko's place?'

'How do you know? We could be from the Tamang monastery.'

'Monks who have still not observed and absorbed could only be those who have disappointed Ekaijinko. Anyway, would you be kind enough to tell the Kameng river that Genkei needs water to wash and cook? I need her to come up to me.'

The monks wondered if Genkei was mad, but they agreed to pass on his message to the river. When the monks got to the Kameng, they said, 'Hi, river. Hope you haven't had a tough day. We have a message for you. Genkei has asked you to meet him at his house because he needs water to cook and wash.' They laughed, thinking that the river would find the request absurd. But suddenly, the Kameng started gurgling louder and louder, as if in response to the monks' words. Before the monks could make sense of this, she turned and twisted, changing her normal course, and started crawling up the hill. The monks were shocked. They couldn't believe their eyes. With mouths open in surprise, they stared at each other and wondered what to do.

'Let's follow her. This has to be magic,' called out Eido, a young monk. They followed the river as she snaked up, until they arrived at Genkei's house. Genkei was busy cleaning the huge deer, and he didn't notice the 100 young monks around him. He clearly hadn't even noticed that the Kameng river had arrived at his house and was now flowing next to his garden like a spirited mountain stream.

'Genkei!' shouted Banzen, a tall monk in the group. 'What are you doing? Are you playing a trick on us? You haven't noticed all of us surrounding you or this river that is making such an awful amount of noise in your garden. Tell us what your secret is.'

The other monks joined in, saying, 'You have to disclose your magic trick to us. You can't hide it any more.'

Genkei looked up and smiled. He did not say a word. The monks waited for an answer, but when Genkei went back to washing his meat without responding to the monks' demand, Banzen got impatient and yelled, 'If you don't tell us, we will take away your meat and pull down your house. You will have nothing left.'

Genkei looked up again and said, 'I am not afraid of you taking away my meat or pulling down my house, but since you are Ekaijinko's students, I will tell you what the secret is.' Genkei picked up the washed meat and placed it on the table. Leaving his veranda, he walked to the river, pressed his palms together and said, 'Thank you for coming to help me, sister. I will return the favour with any help you want from me whenever you so desire.' He then turned to the students and said, 'If you have the resolve to do something, you succeed in doing it. All you need is absolute faith in yourself, and you can achieve even the most impossible things.'

The monks were not satisfied with the explanation. Together they screamed, 'Teach us your secret, Genkei. We can't wait to hear.'

Genkei pointed to the tallest rhododendron tree in the jungle that surrounded his house, and he told them that he learnt the secret by climbing the tree's branches and sitting there in meditation for seven days straight.

'It's not me. It's this tree that has magical powers. That's where I got it,' he said.

The students looked up at the tree and asked Genkei how they could climb it when it was so imposing and tall. Genkei told the monks to use the other trees around the rhododendron to make the tallest ladder possible. This would help them reach the top. The students looked up at the tree and were perplexed. It seemed impossible to climb.

Genkei studied the monks and said, 'Give up? I knew you would. You people are weak and undisciplined. You could never do it.'

Challenged by Genkei in this most humiliating manner, the monks got to work. By late evening, they had made a very tall ladder, which could take them up to the topmost branches of the tree. Without looking at Genkei, who was sitting by the kitchen window, trying to stoke a fire, the monks quickly climbed up the branches. As soon as the last monk had climbed up, Genkei slipped out of his kitchen and took away the ladder from the base of the tree.

The monks were dismayed to see the hunter steal their ladder. They called out to him, 'Genkei, what are you doing? Why are you taking the ladder? How will we come down now?'

But as they urged the hunter to bring back the ladder, they saw Genkei chop up the ladder into smaller parts and use some of the wood to feed his fire. The monks were now convinced that Genkei was seeking revenge for their rude behaviour. After all, they had threatened to break his house. How could a hunter like him take that insult?

Given no choice, the young monks remained on the tree branches, meditating for days without food or water. When their hunger became unbearable, they pleaded with Genkei, seeking forgiveness for their behaviour and asking him to help get them down. Each time they pleaded, Genkei would shout out, 'Jump if you want to. There is no ladder or rope here. Jump, jump, jump.'

The monks looked down and were filled with fear. *We'll turn into a bag of bones if we jump*, the monks thought. Eido, who had been very eager to learn Genkei's magic powers, was petrified. He called out to Banzen and asked, 'What will we do? It has been ten days since we climbed up here. If we don't get to the ground, we will fall because of fatigue. We must convince Genkei to help us.'

Banzen realized that Eido was right. If falling from the tree wouldn't kill them, their hunger surely would. He squeezed his eyes shut, gathered all the power in his lungs and hollered from his branch, 'Genkei, I am ready to do whatever you tell me to do. Please, please have pity on us and help us.' His voice echoed through the mountains and valleys and reached the ears of Master Ekaijinko.

As Banzen opened his eyes, he heard his master's voice saying, 'Observe and absorb.'

He then looked at Genkei, who, having heard Banzen's plea, was shouting, 'Jump, jump, jump!' He then added for the first time, 'Jump and you shall fly!'

Suddenly, Banzen realized what his master had been trying to teach them—control your thoughts or your thoughts will control you. It was the same thing that Genkei had been trying to teach them when he had said, 'If you have the resolve to do something then you succeed in doing it. All you need is absolute faith in yourself, and then you can achieve even the most impossible things.'

Awakened and aware of his own strengths and the power of thought, Banzen decided to try the impossible — he was going to attempt to fly. He said to his fellow students, 'It is better to try flying than die without trying.' Saying this, he spread his arms out and jumped off the tree, his words still ringing in the ears of the other monks. Off the tree and swimming in the air, Banzen's arms were spread like a bird's wings, his crimson robes ballooning in the wind like a parachute, helping him sail. As Banzen skimmed the blue skies like a phoenix, he screeched, 'I can fly!'

The monks could not believe what they were seeing. Banzen had flown like a kite and made a perfect landing on the ground. A moment later, they had all found not only the courage to follow Banzen in his flight but also the conviction to do so. One by one, the monks started jumping off the tree, flying like beautiful red birds, dotting the blue sky and leaving the tree bare. The monks had taken their flight to freedom. There was no fear of the unknown, fear of the impossible or fear of failure. Their egos would no longer punish them if they failed. Master Ekaijinko's last lesson on ego and fear was suddenly spattered across the sky, swimming and sailing. Genkei looked up and saw the shower of red blossoms from above. He had done his job, fulfilling his promise to his old friend, Ekaijinko. The master's students had been trained. As he watched the students glide, Ekaijinko's words came back to him. 'My students must learn that holding on to and nurturing an ego only keeps one chained and servile. To be absolutely free, one must lose ego and fear. You teach them that, Genkei.'

Realizing what they had just been taught by Genkei, the monks, once safely on the ground, bowed to him as a mark of surrender to the wise. They then turned around and started walking back towards the Urgelling monastery to their master.

Even today, when the skies above Mount Gorichen turn crimson, they say that a Genkei is busy teaching patience, fearlessness and an ego-free existence to a group of monks. Mount Gorichen, they say, is often red mixed with ochre in colour.

This story comes from Arunachal Pradesh. It's one of the rarer tales that you 'will hear from the state. Despite the strong Buddhist influence and the revered Tawang monastery, most of the popular tales from the state are 'woven around the daily lives of the villagers from different tribes. This tale gives us a peek into the lives of the monks 'who live and train in this region.

Acknowledgements

This book has come into being because of all those who've taken forward the tradition of storytelling and have kept it alive. We've benefited immensely from existing published sources and unpublished oral traditions while writing these folk tales and would like to thank all these influences.

This book would not have been possible without our parents, Thakur Vishva Narain Singh and Sushila Devi, whose indomitable spirit we have imbibed. Our father, a well-known writer and a Soviet Land Nehru Award winner, was the one to kindle the passion for reading in us, and led us to wander through the world of fables and verses, right through our childhood. We are indebted to him for the endless supply of books at home and egging us on to express ourselves in words. For appreciating every silly rhyme we wrote and prodding us to find, foster and feast on the writer within. And, above all, for giving us the gift to be our own women. We are beholden to our mother, Sushila Devi, a master storyteller and writer, for carving us wings that we could use to fly to wherever we wanted and encouraging us through that flight. For her unflinching support and belief in her daughters, and for strengthening us with her fortitude. She has engaged with us through myths, legends and folk tales, many of which have remained favourite folk tales of our family for generations! We owe to her our constant curiosity for the unknown and the fearlessness to explore unchartered territories. She has taught us to pursue our dreams without compromise and shown us that fulfilling our aspirations requires grit.

Our gratitude also to our Nani ji, Ram Kumari Devi, our original storyteller, who made childhood evenings fascinating with her tales. To our Dada ji, Thakur Beni Madho Singh, whose stories nurtured our childhood fantasies.

We are grateful to our nephew, Raghavendra Ranbir Singh Bisht, for being our captive audience and guinea pig for all our new story ideas. But above all, for being an intelligent and thoughtful mind whose opinion we value. We greatly appreciate his criticism and insight into children's favourite reads, which helped us chisel these stories! We couldn't have finished this book without him and cherish the love and pride he throws into the things we do.

We are also thankful to our sister, Rachna Gahilote Bisht, for stepping in every time one has needed help, supporting us to find that space to write in and loving and endorsing every word that flows from our pens. A big thank you to her for being unfailingly reliable and for supplying us with endless cups of savoury tea!

To Yashwant Bisht, for introducing us to Kumauni culture.

Our gratitude to Mrs B. Gill, for fuelling our abiding romance with the English language and being the best-ever to teach English to countless Dehra girls. We're also thankful to her for her love, her immense knowledge, her impeccable diction, which made English classes unmissable, and showing faith in our abilities. Above all, we are grateful to her for taking a school association beyond the campus and turning us into family. For teaching us by example fortitude, self-reliance, the sense of giving and the magic of a good heart.

Our deep-felt thankfulness to the Himalayas, for releasing a magic in our lives fit for fairy tales, and to authors Paul Brunton, Stephen Alter, Ruskin Bond and Allan Sealy, who constantly fed our never-ending affair of the heart with the Himalayas. To Dehradun, for being just the perfect potion for literary romance and fertile imaginations. To Dehradun's MBD—the Russian Book Depot that made Russian tales a part of our growing years.

To CJM Dehra and its principals, Sr Prudence, Sr Lawrence and Sr Gladys, for their terrific schooling. To Sr Regus, Mr Rick, Mrs S. Srivastava and Mrs E. Kapoor for making school such a wonderfully affectionate place. To Mrs Madhu Vohra and Mrs Reena Dangwal, English teachers from junior and middle school who spent time reading our little scribbles. To Mrs Pubra, Mrs Mohini Sharma and Mrs Nautiyal, Hindi teachers who helped us build a bond with languages. To Mrs Pushpa Bajaj, the school librarian, who never turned down our incessant demand for books and urged us to read more and more. To Alpana Bhagatji, for believing our exaggerated childhood yarns and laughing through them, and Ashwini Bhagatji, for buoying us all through our lives.

To S.K. Misra and Armoogum Parsuramen, for their encouragement and guidance. To Mangalam Swaminathan, dear friend and greatest supporter of our storytelling initiative, Kathakar, who selflessly worked to make storytelling performances a cherished possibility for thousands of children and adults. The world of storytelling is poorer without her.

To Ginger, for making life rich with her boundless, selfless love and pulling us out for walks when we didn't want any! Thank you for also giving us an informed perspective on animal emotions!

We would also like to thank Penguin Random House for sharing our love for the tales from the Himalayas and bringing them to life for our readers. To Nimmy Chacko, our commissioning editor, whose continuous enthusiasm for our work kept us going. To Janaki Sundaram, our copy editor, who meticulously went through all the stories, making them crisper. To Sohini Mitra, for looking after the project so lovingly and tenderly, and turning our dream into a reality. Our thanks also to Jit Chowdhury for visualizing our stories through the lovely illustrations; to Meena Rajasekaran, for a brilliant cover; and to Nisha Singh, for helping our work reach far and wide. This book happened because of this fabulous bunch of people.

Prarthana would also like to acknowledge ace journalist Diptosh Majumdar, for inspiring excellent writing and prompting one to discover newer expressions in language. For encouraging young reporters like her to express themselves through unusual poetry and prose, even while writing journalistic reports, and for being the best editor and adopted father one could find. Dr Anil K. Aggarwal and Major Ravindra Singh Doonga, who cheered her on with every story in print. Sushma Gupta, godmother and friend, for her everlasting affection and encouragement, and Arvind Gupta, for boosting mettle and kindliness. Barrister V.K. Mishra, Rajendra Awasthi, Thakur Kishan Singh, Captain Shoorveer Singh Panwar of Tehri and Lokesh Ohri, for shaping one's mind and influences. And cousins who helped to hone her skill through a ceaseless exchange of letters.

To the fascinatingly independent ladies, Rani Sa'ab Achinta Kumari of Tehri, Mrs Vinod Aggarwal and Sudha L. Kumar for being examples of women's empowerment.

To Shaguna, who thought of this collection, was convinced about the idea of this book and very kindly roped her into her belief.

To her parents-in-law, B.K. Rana and Krishna Rana, for their continued love and blessings.

And finally, to Mohit Chauhan, for putting up with erratic writing hours, providing the creative succour to stitch words into his melodies and, above all, for perpetually chasing her to write a book, insisting that she must. Thank you also for the abundance of live music at home!

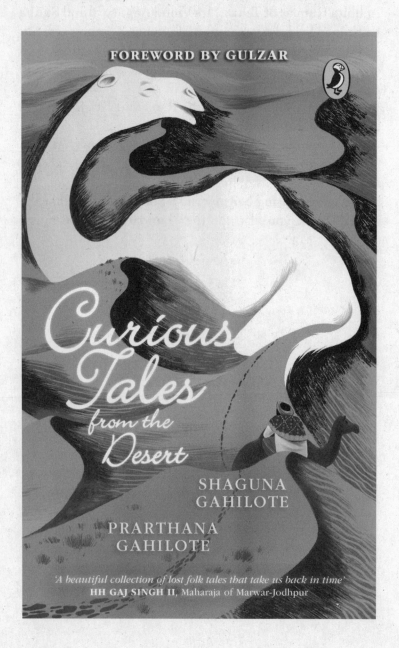

Curious Tales from the Desert

Deep in the wild jungles of Rajasthan resides a magical
sparrow that grants wishes . . .

In Gujarat, a pandit haggles with vendors and chastises
merchants as he chases an elusive bargain . . .

A bullocky in Multan encounters a mysterious and wise old
man who charges money to talk!

A pandemonium of fools, geniuses and everyone in
between gambol across the deserts of India to amusing
and delightful results.

'A beautiful collection of lost folk tales that take
us back in time'
HH GAJ SINGH II, Maharaja of Marwar-Jodhpur

'Beautiful and innocent . . . Took me back to a time when
my grandmother would regale me with folk tales.
Makes me want to fly off once again'
SHANTANU MOITRA

'The stories are ageless and pristine and each one a
remarkable discovery'
IMTIAZ ALI

'Witty, wacky and astounding stories. A book for all ages'
MOHIT CHAUHAN